THE BUTTERFLY DANCE

It's 1902 and life, for Katherine Johnson, has been rather mundane, living with her Aunt Phoebe and Uncle Zachariah in their house on the coast. However, on her twentieth birthday, she meets Kane O'Brien on the beach and suddenly her thoughts are all of him. But will the circumstances of Kane's birth prevent her Aunt from accepting their love for one another? What is the mystery of the beautiful keepsake box? And where will the butterfly dance lead them?

ROSEMARY A. SMITH

THE BUTTERFLY DANCE

Complete and Unabridged

LINFORD
Leicester

First published in Great Britain in 2009

First Linford Edition
published 2010

British Library CIP Data

Smith, Rosemary A.
  The butterfly dance. - -
  (Linford romance library)
  1. Love stories.
  2. Large type books.
  I. Title II. Series
  823.9'2–dc22

  ISBN 978–1–44480–226–9

Published by
F. A. Thorpe (Publishing)
Anstey, Leicestershire

Set by Words & Graphics Ltd.
Anstey, Leicestershire
Printed and bound in Great Britain by
T. J. International Ltd., Padstow, Cornwall

This book is printed on acid-free paper

Written with love in memory
of our beautiful sister
Ruth Thomas
who loved butterflies
and poppy meadows.
In our hearts forever.

1

As I pulled back the heavy yellow brocade curtains in my bedroom, I looked at the pleasant May day scene before me. The sun was rising, casting a warm glow over the sea and lining the distant clouds on the horizon with a bright pink light, holding the promise of a beautiful day.

On the adjacent cliffs, with Monks Bay between us, I could see the imposing grey stone house of Treverrick, which in the early-morning light, appeared far softer and more tranquil than it would do in an hour or so — its many chimneys disappearing and at one with the sky. I knew that the white walls of our home, which I had shared with Aunt Phoebe and Uncle Zachariah since I was a baby, would also be bathed with a translucent light..

'Katherine,' my aunt's voice called

from below the stairs. 'Please come down, we have something for you.'

I moved away from the window and checked my appearance in a full-length mirror that stood on the dark, polished floorboards in one corner by the window of my room. In the half light of morning, my dark wavy hair appeared darker still as it fell loosely around my shoulders. It was 'as black as a raven's wing' Uncle Zac would often say, in his quiet, gentle voice. My shining eyes were grey, set in an unblemished, fair complexion — apart from the small brown mole to the right of my nose.

Stepping back, I ensured that my pale purple gown with capped gathered sleeves and the skirt with an insert of lace falling to my feet, was tidy, for Aunt Phoebe was a stickler for perfection over dressing. She had insisted on us wearing purple in the morning as a sign of respect for Queen Victoria, who had died the previous January.

I had often longed to run across the cliff in gay abandon, as many times I felt restricted by protocol. Little did I know that today, my life would be changed irrevocably and that I would one day soon be my own person.

Descending the narrow wooden staircase, I held my skirts up to avoid tripping over them. The grandfather clock in the narrow hallway showed the time as five minutes to seven, as light started to filter through the long window beside the heavy oak front door. It was all so familiar to me and I made my way instinctively to the large kitchen, with its long, well-scrubbed wooden table, which is where I was sure that my aunt and uncle would be. Before I reached the low door, our maid, Aggie, stepped into the hall, stopping me in my tracks.

'They ain't in there, Miss. For some reason they be in the parlour. I really don't know quite what's going on.' She sniffed and walked on, her blonde curls bobbing beneath her white mop cap. 'Happy Birthday,' she said as an afterthought then climbed the stairs.

Retracing my steps, I walked towards the low door at the bottom of the stairway, my hand on the round, brass knob. I hesitated as I heard Aunt Phoebe's firm voice.

'It is only right that she should have it and that is an end to it, Zachariah Johnson.' At these words, all was quiet so I entered the room. My aunt and uncle were standing at the table, which stood beneath the large window, the sun already casting a strip of light across the oak dresser opposite, with the blue and white china standing as it always had for as long as I can remember. Nothing had changed in twenty years, except that Aunt Phoebe had started to grey at the temples. Her startling, violet eyes fixed on me as I stood there, they almost matched the purple gown she wore.

Something was different today. I couldn't explain it, but a heavy atmosphere of uncertainty hung in the air and my dear uncle shuffled from one foot to the other, the morning light shining on his bald head and rounded figure. My usually confident aunt wrung her hands in front of her with a nervous gesture.

'Many happy returns, Katherine!' She walked towards me and embraced me. 'Say something, Zachariah,' she said impatiently to her husband.

'I wish you Happy Birthday also, my dear!' he commenced, pausing to cough. 'We have something for you,' he continued, indicating an object covered with a white tray cloth that sat on the table.

'Well, look at it child, please,' Aunt Phoebe said with some impatience as I stood there looking from one to the other.

Slowly, I walked to the table and lifted the tray cloth from the object beneath. I gasped with delight! It was a rectangular box, but no ordinary box. I ran my hand gently across the beautifully decorated lid on which lay glazed porcelain pink roses with little rosebuds escaping each side to the edge. Each corner of the box was gilded intricately like lace with tiny hearts of pink porcelain interspersed here and there, and on each side of the rosewood box was a small miniature decorated with richly coloured flowers.

'Lift the lid, child,' my Aunt encouraged.

I did as I was bid and could see the interior was as rich as the lid, lined with pink silk velvet, on which lay a string of creamy pearls with a diamond clasp and other small items, including a gold needle case. I looked at my aunt and uncle.

'Thank you both so much! I have never seen anything so exquisite and the pearls,' I continued, overcome with the richness of the whole gift, 'they are quite lovely.'

Lifting them from the box with trembling hands, I attempted to place them around my neck.

'Let me help you,' Uncle Zac said, at last moving from the spot he had been transfixed to since I had entered the room. The pearls in place around my throat, I hugged them both and gently closed the lid of the box. The room was suddenly quiet.

'Tell her, Zachariah, go on,' Aunt Phoebe urged in her dominant forthright manner. 'Tell me what?' I asked, somewhat confused.

'The pearls are a gift from us, but they're . . . ' he faltered momentarily. 'The keepsake box and its contents are your birthright.'

'What do you mean?' I questioned, now more perplexed than ever.

'It is an object handed down in the family and we thought that your twentieth birthday would be a good time to present it to you,' Aunt Phoebe explained.

'I see,' I said quietly, not really seeing at all, but at that moment, looking at the delightful object on the table, I was just thankful that it now belonged to me.

'Now that is cleared up, let us take breakfast together,' my aunt said cheerfully, suddenly seeming more herself. In truth, everything seemed normal again, even Uncle Zac who took me by my arm as we made our way to the kitchen.

'The gypsies are back again, Mistress,' Aggie said as she placed the toast rack in front of us. 'In the field behind Treverrick, they are,' she continued, folding her arms and standing over us awaiting my aunt's reply. Aggie was older than me by nine years and she had been with us at Northcliffe House for ten. While her manner was abrupt, she had a good heart and was very loyal.

'It is the right time of year, Aggie. Now continue with your tasks, my dear, while we finish breakfast,' Aunt Phoebe said firmly.

As Aggie did as she was bid, my aunt turned her attention to me while buttering a piece of toast.

'We have another pleasant surprise for you, Katherine,' she whispered with a sparkle in her eyes.

8

'Another? What is it, Aunt, please tell me?' I exclaimed.

'We are to dine at Treverrick this evening for it is Constance Trevartha's birthday also and they are to have a small gathering in celebration. The invitation arrived last week while you were out walking. You can wear your new cream gown for the occasion.' Aunt Phoebe didn't stop for breath. 'Daniel and Nicholas will be there my dear, now what do you say?' she asked of me.

'That is indeed a wonderful surprise, Aunt,' I replied meekly, for while I had in the past, on several occasions, enjoyed afternoon tea at Treverrick, in their opulent drawing room, the thought of my Aunt's matchmaking filled me with dread for I wished to find my own husband and should I remain a spinster then so be it.

'Splendid,' my aunt enthused. 'Now, I suggest you take a walk in the morning air and bring some colour to those pallid cheeks.'

9

* * *

Back in my bedroom, I placed the keepsake box on my dressing table, once more admiring the beauty and perfection of it. I unclasped the pearls from around my neck and lifted the lid of the box to replace them on the pink silk, as I thought about my uneventful life so far.

I had learned to dance and ride horses amongst other genteel pastimes at the Academy For Young Women in Truro, where I spent three years from the age of sixteen. While it was beautiful living here on the coast of Cornwall, where would I meet the husband I envisaged? I could understand Aunt Phoebe's desire to manoeuvre a match for me with a son of Treverrick, but today I would not think of such things. It was my birthday and I would go walking — a thing I loved to do for it gave me the sense of freedom I craved. Gently I shut the lid of the keepsake box, vowing to discover its contents later.

My bedroom was not a large room, but comfortable none the less — the feather mattress on my small bed with the pale-yellow crocheted cover inviting me each evening to snuggle down for the night. I had never spent a restless night in that comfortable bed. Little did I know that was all to change. Going to the wardrobe I took out the purple cape that matched my gown, draping it around my shoulders and tying the ribbon at the neck. Quickly, I looked into the mirror, twisting my hair into a knot at the nape of my neck and placing my purple and white bonnet on my head. I was ready to go, anxious to be out in the sunlight and breathing in the salty sea air.

Stepping out of the door on to the path, lined each side by a lawn, I walked to the gate, stopping to look out over the sea. The sun had risen higher and the water now appeared as a mass of sparkling diamonds.

Walking to a field on the right, I went to greet my brown mare Minnie, who hung her head over the gate, waiting for some show of affection as she did each day. I rewarded her with a sugar lump and then walked down the narrow path on the cliff, heading for Monks Cove. The tide was out at the moment, water lapping gently on the sand over the rocks, but in a couple of hours, the sandy cove would be swallowed up in a torrent of water and the waves would be pounding against the cliffs.

Treading on the firm sand of the cove, I could see someone on the far side heading towards me. It was a man and I muttered an oath as I had wished to be alone, however, I carried on walking, every now and then stooping to pick up pebbles and nonchalantly throwing them in the water.

The stranger drew nearer and stopped about a foot in front of me. His hair was as black as coal, curling around his neck and face, and his black glittering eyes surveyed me from a handsome, tanned face. He wore a white blouson shirt open at the neck, which accentuated his dark skin. I didn't know what to say, my colour deepening as I realised that I was gazing at him boldly.

'Good morning, lovely lady, it is a glorious day!' He spoke in a rich, deep voice.

'It is, indeed,' I managed to utter.

'And all the more glorious for me to have encountered you,' he said brightly.

'Why, thank you,' I replied, quite cross with myself for stumbling over a few simple words.

'May I be so bold as to ask who you are?' he questioned, holding my eyes with his own as he spoke.

'You may be so bold, Sir.' I laughed, feeling more confident by the second. 'My name is Katherine Johnson and I live at Northcliffe House,' I offered, waving one gloved hand in the direction of my home, which now looked like a white miniature house in the distance.

'Do you ride, Katherine Johnson?' the stranger asked suddenly, taking me by surprise.

'I do, indeed. I have a lovely gentle

mare called Minnie,' I told him.

'Then you shall ride with me tomorrow to Lands End,' he instructed. 'I shall meet you by the Chapel field at ten o'clock tomorrow morning. Let us hope for a fine day.'

Before I could answer, he had turned on his heel, retracing his steps and leaving me wondering what had happened to me in such a short space of time, for I didn't want him to go and I felt lonely without him there. My desire was to run after him, but decorum prevented it. Then, I realised I had not asked his name, but for some reason he no longer seemed like a stranger. All day, thoughts of him filled my head and I knew that on the morrow, I would do as he had bid and ride with him for I longed to be in his company.

'You are day dreaming today,' Aunt Phoebe observed that afternoon, 'but it is your birthday and you are no doubt looking forward to this evening.'

I hadn't the heart to tell her that the last thing I wanted to do was dine at

Treverrick that evening. All I wished to do was converse with the handsome stranger. Then the thought came to me that he may not keep our assignation and hot tears pricked my eyes.

Reluctantly, I prepared myself that evening with Aggie's help. My new cream-coloured gown with a strip of pink roses on one side, slipped over my head and fell smoothly in place. The bodice was also decorated with small pink flowers. Aggie arranged my dark hair with tendrils falling each side of my face and then she secured two pink flowers to one side of my head.

'Just the pearls now, Aggie, thank you,' I said, lifting the lid of the keepsake box, longing at that moment to look through the contents but knowing I would have to wait until the morrow.

'Miss Katherine!' Aggie exclaimed as she clasped the pearls around my neck. 'What a beautiful box, would that I had one like it.'

'Yes, I am extremely fortunate. It is

beautiful, isn't it?' I agreed, closing the lid once more. 'Now, I must meet my aunt and uncle downstairs, for I am sure they are impatient to leave.'

We walked to Treverrick, as no carriage would traverse the field we had to cross. It was a warm evening and as we walked I glanced down at the cove, thinking briefly of my meeting with the stranger that morning. Treverrick looked larger and more formidable with each step we took towards it. As we walked up the short drive, I stopped to look at the front of the rambling grey building which commanded a view of the sea, its leaded windows glinting like a row of glowing candles in the light of the evening sun. Involuntarily, I shuddered thinking how I'd loathe to live here. I much preferred our cosy white house on the adjacent cliff, which from here, looked like a dolls' house awaiting our return.

We stepped into the vast stone-flagged hall which appeared cold and

uninviting, with suits of armour standing against the walls, seeming grey and
harsh in the half light. The huge
fireplace was cold and still and I
shuddered again. The only thing with
any appeal was the wide, curving
staircase with a polished banister and
red carpet, almost beckoning me to the
upper floor. Our capes removed and
carried away by an elderly man-servant,
we were shown into the drawing room
by a young maid wearing a black dress
and starched white cap and apron.

'Mr and Mrs Johnson!' a loud
enthusiastic voice exclaimed, 'and
young Katherine, although not so
young now. Indeed, a beautiful young
woman and it is your birthday as well
as mine. How charming you look!
Now, let me introduce you to my
sister Patience.'

The two virtues stood together,
Constance Trevartha, once a Treverrick,
overshadowing her shy, retiring sister,
who I believed was a Miss and had only
lately returned to Treverrick. Constance

wore an emerald-green dress full of lace, ribbons and flowers of various colours, quite overpowering like the woman herself.

Patience, on the other hand, wore a pale grey dress, trimmed delicately at the neck and wrists with cream lace. She nodded her dark head in acknowledgement of us. The sisters were both dark and surprisingly young, although I guessed Patience to be the younger of the two.

'Now, Katherine, come and say hello to my two sons, Daniel and Nicholas as you have not seen them much of late,' Constance said, leading me towards the two brothers who were standing to one side of the opulent marble fireplace. Everything about the room was full of splendour from the rich maroon curtains at the windows to the sparkling crystal chandelier, which hung from the white decorated ceiling.

'Welcome to Treverrick,' Daniel said. After the vibrancy of my stranger, I could only see him as insipidly handsome with a soft, silky brown moustache and a goatee beard that matched his thin, mousy hair.

Nicholas, however, had matured nicely and was more arresting. He had his mother's dark hair and was clean-shaven, also possessing the smile of an angel. I smiled back at him, thinking that maybe I would enjoy this evening after all, when there was a commotion behind me. The door burst open.

'Forgive me for being late,' a familiar voice said. I turned to face the latecomer and our eyes met across the room. It was none other than my stranger on the beach.

2

'Aunt Phoebe, who was that young man?' I asked at breakfast next morning.

'Which young man?' my aunt replied, her toast hovering at her mouth but never quite reaching it.

'The stranger,' I queried insistently, knowing full well my aunt knew who I was talking about.

'That is Kane,' she replied, her toast being laid back on her plate. 'He is a gypsy and I would ask that you have nothing to do with him.'

'If I am not to have anything to do with him, why was he at Treverrick last night?' I protested. 'The family seemed to welcome him with open arms.'

'They welcomed him because he saved their son Daniel, a couple of years ago, from a watery grave,' my aunt explained, 'and now, each time the gypsies come and camp behind the big house, Kane is invited to take dinner with the family. But that does not mean that you can associate with him and that is my final word,' she finished emphatically.

What would my aunt think, I mused, if she knew I was meeting this handsome stranger this very morning?

As I made my way to feed the hens in the back yard, I knew that I would not adhere to my aunt's wishes. As I scattered the corn from the galvanised bucket, which I held tucked under my arm, I felt suddenly very much alive and carefree. I'd even changed into my oldest pale green cotton gown, the skirts feeling cool around me. I hummed as I distributed the seed, casting it over the patchy ground, the hens peck-pecking away and suddenly my bucket was empty. Swinging the handle over my arm, I looked out over the sea which shimmered in the early morning light, my mind on the handsome stranger called Kane, knowing that I could hardly wait to see him, see those black eyes that spoke to me.

A short while later, I was astride Minnie, bareback, my senses acute, as I made my way to the Chapel field. I had heard Aunt Phoebe's voice calling me.

'Katherine, where are you going dressed like that and no saddle? Katherine!' she shouted, but I chose to ignore her, for today, I would do as I wanted and not as I was bid.

Kane was not there and disappointment surged through me. I could feel the May sun beating down on my forearms and at the neckline of my cool gown. I looked around me and even as I looked, I could see Kane riding towards me, at one with his huge black horse.

'Katherine,' he greeted me as he pulled his mount to a halt alongside me. There were to be no formalities with Kane and I welcomed it. Minnie trotted sedately alongside Kane's horse, Thunder. I felt the breeze on my skin and in my hair, hair that was as black as Kane's. For the first time I felt free, away from stuffy drawing rooms and protocol. Kane and I needed few words between us as we rode in a companionable silence until we reached the clearing behind Treverrick.

'Does the sight before you please you?' Kane asked as we pulled up our mounts. What lay before us was a circle of four brightly painted caravans, with men and women sat on the steps, the men smoking pipes and the women preparing what looked like vegetables, in the open air. A fire had been lit in the midst of it all, the pale plume of blue smoke spiralling gently towards the sky.

'Yes,' I answered him, 'it does please me, for I have never seen such a calm scene before in my life.'

'Would you like to meet my mother?' Kane asked, his eyes sparkling. For only a moment, I hesitated before replying,

'Yes, that would be nice,' I told him.

We both reined our horses to a tree, me feeding Minnie a sugar lump and reassuring her as I whispered in her ear. Kane took my arm as if it were the most natural thing to do and I gave no resistance as he led me over to the brightest wagon where, at the top of the steps, each side of the door had been painted with red and green scrolls, bearing the name 'Tessa and Jed'.

As we got nearer, the woman looked up and smiled. She was beautiful, with coal black hair falling in waves to her waist. Although her teeth were yellowing, it did not detract from the dazzling smile she gave us as she stopped what she was doing and stood up to greet us.

'And who might this be?' she asked Kane.

'This, Mother, is Katherine and I shall marry her.'

His words took me completely by surprise and I felt the colour suffuse my cheeks.

'There now, you've embarrassed the dear child, Kane,' she said, taking my arm. 'You really should think before you speak, Son,' she admonished him.

'I have thought of nothing else but her since yesterday,' Kane replied.

'Take no notice, Kate, and come with me.' Kane's mother led me up the steps of the wagon and the name by which she called me seemed so right that I did not challenge it.

The interior of the caravan was smaller than I'd imagined it to be, but furnished to perfection. Two beds, one above the other, occupied the back of the wagon where pristine white sheets, edged with the most exquisite crochet work, peeped over the top of woollen blankets. Everything was so clean and the woodwork was highly polished.

A glass cabinet held a delightful porcelain tea service, the pink cups embellished with pink roses, which caused me to think of the keepsake box and home. What would Aunt Phoebe say, I mused as I took in everything before me? But the truth was, I didn't care. Although I'd been happy all these years in the white house by the sea, I felt as if I belonged here and had waited for this moment all of my life.

'Do you like what you see, Katherine?'

Kane asked from the bottom of the steps, interrupting my thoughts.

'Of course she does, don't you, Kate?' Kane's mother said.

I don't know what I'd expected from a gypsy encampment, but it certainly wasn't like the picture I'd built up in my mind. Tessa, if indeed she was called Tessa, was dressed simply in a black poplin skirt with a white blouse open at the neck, which revealed her tanned skin. A black belt, interwoven with red and yellow flowers, encircled her tiny waist. So simple, yet so lovely, was my thought, as she led me back down the steps.

'Here's a knife,' she said, handing me the small black handled tool, 'you can help me peel these potatoes for supper, Kate' and as she spoke, I did as I was bid, sitting alongside her on the bottom step of the wagon.

As I looked around, I could see that every caravan had high wheels with the main body of the wagon perched on top, but each one was as beautifully painted and carved as the other. As I glanced here and there, a man tossed a large piece of wood on the fire, sending the smoke even higher and the sparks flying around it.

'Where do you draw your water from?' I asked Kane's mother.

'From the stream over there,' she informed me, eyeing me with amusement and pointing to a small stream, which ran alongside the clearing.

The potatoes done, Tessa picked up the bowl we'd placed them in and tucking it under her arm, beckoned me to follow her. She led me to the caravan behind her own, where I could see a large cauldron pot sitting on the ground by the steps. It was already nearly filled with a variety of food. The young woman who sat on the steps, acknowledged me with a smile and my thought was that she had to be Kane's sister, for the resemblance between Tessa and this young woman was uncanny.

'This is my daughter, Maddy,' Tessa announced, as if reading my thoughts and as she spoke, she laid the bowl of potatoes on the ground by the cauldron.

'Hello, Maddy,' I acknowledged the pretty girl. 'My name is Kate.'

'And our Kane has a wish to marry her,' Tessa added then threw back her head and laughed.

'Why do you laugh so?' I asked her, quite put out by her merriment.

'Because Kane has never wanted to marry anyone,' Maddy explained. 'Isn't that right, Mother?'

'It certainly is, but then, he's never before spoken of it either,' Tessa said seriously.

'And would you marry my brother?' Maddy asked me.

The question had me at a disadvantage, for I had only met Kane yesterday, but I trembled at his nearness and felt I had known him a lifetime already.

'I cannot answer that,' I said quietly, 'not for the moment at least.'

The conversation was abruptly cut short, when a young man, who was obviously Maddy's husband, arrived with a pail of water.

'Is it ready?' he asked, nodding in my direction.

'We have yet to cut up the potatoes,' Tessa answered, 'but please say hello to Kate.'

'Welcome! I'm Isaac,' the young man said.

Tessa, Maddy and I set to cutting up the potatoes and mixing them with the other ingredients in the large pot. When we were finished, Isaac poured the contents of his bucket over the food and lifting the cauldron by its handle, he carried it to the fire, where the men folk had set up a pole with a branch to hang the cauldron on and it was left to cook.

'Will you join us for supper?' Tessa asked.

'Thank you for asking me, but I shall have to return home for lunch or Aunt Phoebe will worry as to where I am. On the morrow, I can visit again, if that is all right?' I asked.

'Don't leave it too long for we shall be moving on in a few days,' Tessa replied.

My heart sank at her words, for I had not even thought of them leaving, which they would do for sure, for they were travellers.

'I shall return tomorrow,' I promised.

'Will you, indeed?' a voice behind me said and I turned to see Kane watching the scene before him, a scene I already felt part of. His coal black eyes were sparkling and he held one strong hand out to me and I took it willingly.

'I must go home,' I told him as I felt his hand gently squeeze mine.

Farewells were said and before I knew it, I was astride Minnie once more as Kane accompanied me to the Chapel field where we both pulled our mounts to a halt.

'I can ride with you to your home?' Kane offered.

'It would be better to say farewell here,' I told him, thinking of Aunt Phoebe's words only a few hours ago.

We said goodbye and as I watched Kane and Thunder disappear in the distance, my heart ached. But for what — Kane, the freedom of life in the encampment, or both?

The hallway was cool as I headed for the kitchen, unaware of time and wondering if I had missed lunch. As I opened the kitchen door, I could see my Aunt and Uncle were seated at the table, with Aggie hovering by the kitchen range. Aunt Phoebe stood up when she saw me.

'Where have you been, young woman? Lunch is already late for we have waited for you, in vain it would seem,' my aunt shouted me.

'I apologise for being late,' I said meekly, taking my seat at the table.

'I've never known you so wilful,' Aunt Phoebe observed. 'And I thank you not to ignore me in future when I call to you. Your uncle and I pray it is a solitary incident, don't we, Zac?' she said, turning to look from me to my poor uncle. 'Please speak, Zachariah!'

31

'Let it be a solitary incident, Katherine,' he pleaded, taking my hand and squeezing it, causing me to think of Kane.

'There,' Aunt Phoebe said, seating herself. 'Now let us eat our lunch. Serve the soup, please Aggie, for thank the Lord, we are all here now.'

Aggie ladled the soup in the bowls and as she served mine, I could see her looking at me with sympathy in her eyes and I knew that I would have an ally in this woman.

The day lingered unbearably. My only thoughts were of Kane and his family, wondering if they were yet partaking in the meal that I had helped to prepare. I retired to bed early, pleading a headache, whereas all I really wanted was to be alone with my thoughts.

As I entered my room and lit the lamp on my bedside table, I spotted the keepsake box and decided to look through the contents. As I lifted it down, I could barely believe it was only yesterday my dear aunt and uncle had presented it to me. The glazed roses and rosebuds lay perfectly on the lid, looking as if they were ready to pluck. Where the light from the lamp fell, it looked as if they had been washed with raindrops.

Gently, I laid the box on the table by the lamp and sitting on the bed, I inspected it more closely. It was a deep box and yet the interior had not seemed to be such. The intricate gilding carried on from the top of the beautiful box down each side of the lid and the base, all in the same theme of lace scattered with the tiny fragile looking pink porcelain hearts. The four oval shaped motifs on each side were edged with fancy gilding and each held a painted picture of a different flower. I looked at each in turn.

The first was a red rose in full bloom and as I turned the box around, I could see pink dog roses, red daisies and blue forget-me-nots. All were beautifully crafted with vivid colours. As I opened the lid, it swung back resting on perfect brass hinges. I took the pearls and placed them gently on the table, then lifted out each item in turn. The first thing I held in my hand was the lovely slim gold needle case. Removing the top, I could see it held three sewing needles of various sizes.

Putting the lid back on, I placed the case on my bed and took out the next three items in turn, which indeed, matched perfectly. There was a hair comb made of silver, decorated with tiny pink beads. The pillbox and tiny hand mirror were of silver also, with the same ornamentation. I placed each item in turn on the bed. A silver thimble was the next object I held in my hand and slipping it on my finger, realised with some amazement, it was a perfect fit.

The last thing to lay in the exquisite keepsake box was a length of pink satin ribbon. I lifted it out and ran it through my fingers, to and fro, wondering all the while who this box had belonged to before me and reaching the conclusion that whoever it was, she was a lover of sewing and the pink ribbon was a length not needed and so saved for another occasion. Returning each item to lay once more on the pink satin, I then held the box with the lid open, still marvelling at its beauty. Closing the lid, I returned it to stand once more on my dressing table.

'Who did you belong to?' I wondered aloud. I would probably never know.

I was thirsty so I made my way back down the stairs just as the grandfather clock in the hall was chiming the hour of ten o'clock. Opening the kitchen door, I could see Aggie sitting on a chair by the fire, which burned in the black leaded range. All was still and quiet, a gas lamp burning on one wall, casting a soothing light.

'It's unusual to see you so late, Miss Katherine,' Aggie observed.

'It's a drink I'm seeking,' I told her and as I spoke, the woman got to her feet and poured me a glass of lemonade.

'If I may say, Miss, I felt awful sorry for you earlier today,' Aggie said. 'I've never known you to be late before' she continued, taking her seat once more by the fire.

'If I tell you where I was, Aggie, please don't breathe a word to anyone.' I took an impulsive decision to trust this young woman, for at least I would have someone to talk to.

'I promise, Miss, on my life, I do,' she vowed and I chose to believe her.

'I was at the gypsy encampment,' I divulged, whether rightly or wrongly, I had yet to find out.

Aggie didn't speak for a few minutes and I waited with bated breath for a response.

'If that's what pleases you, Miss, who am I to say anything against it?' the woman said. 'But remember, they'll be gone before you know it.'

As I lay in my comfortable bed that night, tossing and turning, I thought of Aggie's words and felt they were a warning. Then I thought of Kane and knew I would throw caution to the wind for him. I wished with all my heart I was lying between those white sheets with the deep crocheted edge in Tessa's caravan.

3

The next morning, still dressed in my purple gown with a white apron, my hair loose and tumbling down my back, I was collecting the eggs in a wicker basket when Aunt Phoebe called me.

'Katherine, please come indoors for we have a visitor.' Her voice was shrill and full of excitement and left me wondering who the illustrious visitor could be.

'I'll just finish gathering the eggs,' I shouted back to her and uttered an oath for I wished to be on my way to see Kane's family.

'You'll come now, please, child,' Aunt Phoebe instructed and the tone of her voice would broach no argument. Going through the kitchen door I laid my basket on the table.

'They be in the dining room, Miss Katherine,' Aggie informed me, so I walked along the hallway and could indeed hear voices as I approached the door. The strange voice was a masculine one and my heart skipped a beat as I thought of Kane, but the idea soon vanished, as I knew without doubt my aunt would not entertain him in the dining room or the kitchen for that matter.

As I entered the room, the sunlight obscured my vision momentarily and as my eyes adjusted, I could see it was Nicholas Trevartha sitting on the settle by the fireplace and my heart sank.

'Good morning, Miss Johnson,' the visitor said rising from his seat and indicating that I should take his place, which I ignored.

'Hello, Mr Trevartha,' was all I replied, for I did not wish to encourage this young man. He was handsome, right enough, but he did not have the masculine charm of Kane. In fact, I felt nothing at all at the sight of him and in truth, wished him gone.

'I'll arrange for coffee to be brought

in for us,' Aunt Phoebe suddenly said. 'Pull up a chair, Zachariah,' she instructed my uncle, who immediately sat on one of the high-backed dining chairs and I realised that thankfully, he was going to be my chaperone.

There was an awkward silence as my Aunt left the room and I decided to sit on the settle, as I felt conspicuous hovering near the doorway. I realised, that this was not a good move when having seated myself, Nicholas sat down beside me.

'What brings you here, Sir?' I asked, looking him straight in the eye while all I could think of was escaping to the gypsy encampment.

'I've come to ask if you would do me the honour of walking out with me?' Nicholas explained.

At that moment my aunt came back in to the room, with Aggie close at her heels, carrying a large tray laden with a coffee pot, cups and saucers.

'Now, isn't that nice of the young man?' Aunt Phoebe cajoled as she sat on another dining chair. 'That will be all, thank you, Aggie, you may leave us.'

Aggie was intrigued, but left the room.

'Well, answer the young man,' Aunt Phoebe urged and I knew I had to be honest.

'I am so very flattered by your request, Mr Trevartha, but at this moment, I must say no.' I noticed that my aunt looked aghast at my reply, the silver coffee pot in mid-air as she prepared to berate me.

'Katherine, how can you be so rude? I really despair of you these past few days. I feel sure if Nicholas had asked you a week ago, you would have agreed to his charming request.'

I knew that her words were true.

'I am truly sorry' I said rising to my feet, 'but I am not feeling quite myself today. If you will all excuse me, please.'

I lifted my skirt, fleeing from the room and as I hurried along the corridor to the kitchen, I could hear Aunt Phoebe's voice calling me. I rushed past a bewildered Aggie, out into the open once more. My heart was pounding as I headed for Monks Cove, practically running and I realised that I was indeed trying to escape from all that I had known and loved, heading for the unknown and who knew what, but Kane and his family, in those brightly painted wagons, were the only thing I could think of and it dawned on me that to be with them was all I desired.

Walking across the beach, and breathing in the tangy salt sea air, calmed me and I realised that I still wore my white apron. This realisation caused me to giggle, my black hair still flowing down my back to my waist. It was a glorious day, the sun shining on the sea, with a heat haze in the distance, which hovered over the water on the far horizon. The sky was a deep blue with tiny white fluffy clouds scudding across it. It was, indeed, a perfect morning.

I looked to the other end of the

beach, but today, there was no handsome stranger walking toward me and I felt a great sense of disappointment, but I would walk to the clearing behind Treverrick and once again be completely carefree and alive.

As I reached the edge of the encampment, a small dog bounded towards me and sat at me feet and I bent to fuss him, stroking his head. He was mainly white, with small black patches and proved to be very friendly.

'Domino!' one of the men called to him and he bounded back as I made my way to Tessa's caravan. As I reached it, Tessa appeared at the top of the steps.

'Kate!' she exclaimed. 'So you've returned and I guess you wish to see my son. He is with his father, collecting kindling and will be pleased you have come. In the meantime, will you share a coffee with me?'

This request caused me to think of Aunt Phoebe and the silver coffee pot and I felt a pang of guilt, which quickly passed. Tessa and I sat, this time, at the top of the steps, drinking coffee from tin mugs and it was good, good to be in the open air.

'Katherine,' a voice called and I knew straight away — it was Kane. He appeared at the bottom of the steps and my heart bounced so hard in my chest, I thought Tessa would surely hear it. 'You are a wonderful sight to behold, even with your pinafore on,' he joked.

'Hello, Kane,' I managed to utter.

'You could not keep away, then?' he observed.

'It would seem not,' I told him.

'Do not be so bold with the girl,' Tessa chided him, 'you will frighten her away.'

'Never!' said Kane emphatically. 'She is one of us at heart, aren't you, Kate?'

At these words, I didn't quite know how to answer.

'I do love it here.'

'A good answer,' Kane observed. 'Would you like to walk with me and Domino?'

'I would, indeed, but have no bonnet to wear and I don't wish the sun to burn me any more than it has already,' I told him.

'I have a straw bonnet you can borrow, Kate,' Tessa offered as she got to her feet and went into the caravan, coming out a minute later with a wide-brimmed straw hat that was decorated with colourful flowers of blues and yellows. We had enjoyed some merriment as I tried it on. It fitted perfectly and would keep the midday sun from my face.

'So you will walk with me, Kate?' Kane put his hand out to me. and I negotiated the steps toward him, taking the hand he offered.

As we walked past the fire, which burned gently in the clearing, I noticed a red-haired man bending over, stacking small pieces of wood behind one of the wagons. As I watched, he stood up straight, stretching his back.

'So this is the *gorgio*?' he asked, somewhat gruffly to Kane.

'This is Katherine, Father,' Kane told the man. He looked nothing like my companion — Kane was tall, but his father was no taller than me. I looked at Kane.

'What does he mean by a *gorgio*?'

'It is our language for a non-gypsy girl. Don't take too much notice of my sire's gruff manner, for he means no harm,' Kane said gently, but I could not help feeling alarmed at his father's manner and what seemed like hostility.

'I take it you are going walking?' Jed enquired, bending once more to stack some logs.

'We are taking Domino with us,' Kane answered, whistling for the small dog to follow us. Domino raced to his side and we set off.

As we walked hand in hand, it seemed strange but pleasant to me, for I was more used to taking a gentleman's arm. I could see the horses grazing on the grass behind the clearing and then we stepped into a small wood where the sun fell intermittently between the trees. We walked in silence, except for the snapping of twigs beneath our feet, while Domino ran on in front of us, barking as Kane threw him a stick to fetch.

We stepped out of the small wood and found ourselves in a meadow. The grass was quite long, but we followed a path, which had been formed by many feet walking this way. All I could see were red poppies growing in abundance all over the meadow and I felt so carefree that I laughed out loud and caused Kane to stop walking.

'Why do you laugh, Katherine?' he asked in a serious tone.

'Because I am deliriously happy,' I informed him, squeezing the hand which held mine.

'Turn back and look behind you,' he urged as we reached the far end of the meadow.

I turned and realised we had walked up quite a steep incline, although it had not seemed like it at the time. The view behind us was delightful, red poppies swayed in the summer breeze and I could see the wood and behind it, the grey walls of Treverrick, which served to remind me of Nicholas' visit that very morning and a cloud suddenly passed over my happiness.

'You are sure you are happy?' Kane queried, a worried tone in his voice.

'Of course I am,' I told him gaily. 'For what more could I want than the sunshine, summer breeze and to be walking with you.'

'What more, indeed.' he said, smiling once more and we strolled on for what seemed no distance at all, yet we had walked through field after field, until we could see the sea in the distance, as calm as a millpond, appearing golden in the sunlight.

'We must turn back, Katherine, for we have walked quite a distance.'

I realised how hot my feet were and how I longed for a drink. As if reading my mind, Kane drew a bottle filled with water from his pocket and handed it to me. The liquid quenched my thirst and

I handed the glass bottle back to him and he also drank from it, just as a butterfly hovered around us.

'It is a Red Admiral,' Kane said as he noticed my interest in the beautiful creature.

'See, it is black with a vivid flash of orange-red and a splatter of white spots.' As he spoke, two more started to encircle us, wending themselves in and around us.

'It is like a butterfly dance,' I said to him, entranced by the spectacle.

Kane unexpectedly put an arm around me and twirled me around on the spot as we danced with the three Red Admirals. I was breathless when we eventually stopped and Kane took my hands in his. 'Marry me, Katherine.'

I instinctively wanted to say yes, but I paused.

'My aunt and uncle would never allow it,' I sadly told him.

'We can marry at the camp tomorrow,' he insisted.

'I cannot do so without Uncle

Zachariah and Aunt Phoebe's permission.'

'Then I shall ask them, for that is the right thing to do,' he told me.

'And where will we live?' I asked, practicality suddenly taking over.

'In our own *vardo*,' he replied.

'And what is a *vardo*?'

'It is the gypsy word for a caravan, little one.' Kane laughed as he pulled me towards him, the butterflies resuming their dance around us. I was suddenly carefree again, as we whirled around in the field, with the sea in the distance, the sun high in the sky and Domino racing around us.

As we walked back, hand in hand, our footsteps quicker than they were before, we derived a plan that Kane would come to Northcliffe House that evening and ask Uncle Zachariah for my hand in marriage. I knew in my heart, that Uncle Zac would not give his blessing for such a union and then what would we do? Kane sensed my fears.

'If your uncle will not agree, will you still wish to marry me?'

I had to weigh up all the facts before I answered. I wanted nothing more than to marry Kane and share his life travelling the country, carving wooden pegs and weaving baskets for a living, but what if Uncle Zac wouldn't give his consent? At this thought and in answer to Kane's question, I stopped in my tracks amongst the poppies.

'Do you believe in love at first sight?' I asked him.

'I do now,' he answered with a grin. 'If you'd have asked me a week ago, I would have said no.'

'Then let us marry without consent,' I suggested passionately. 'For once the deed is done, it cannot be gone back on.'

'I would feel happier if I asked your uncle first,' Kane admitted seriously.

'No,' I said emphatically. 'I already know what his answer would be.'

'Very well,' he agreed and pushed the straw hat back from my face and bent to kiss me briefly on the lips — a kiss, that was like the touch of a butterfly.

There was great excitement amongst the women of the camp. Tessa and Maddy both hugged me and danced around me with the other two women, who were older, but still very agile.

'And what will you wear?' Maddy asked.

'I shall wear my cream-coloured skirt and orange short-sleeved blouse,' I said, thinking of the Red Admiral butterflies. 'I'd like a circle of poppies in my hair.'

'Perfect!' Tessa shrieked, clapping her hands.

'And what of a priest?' I asked, thinking now of more practical things.

'There will be no need for a priest,' Kane's voice said behind me.

'No priest? Then who will marry us?' I said, somewhat aghast.

'We marry ourselves, in front of everyone here,' he explained. 'But first, we both jump over a besom made of flowering broom and then, after we have made our vow to one another, we share and break the cup of love.'

At Kane's words, I must have looked crestfallen, for Tessa put an arm around me.

'If you are to be with us, Kate, then you will have to abide by our way of life,' she said kindly.

'But of course,' I agreed, smiling once more.

'No good will come of it, bringing a *gorgio* into the family,' Jed's gruff voice bellowed. I gave him a dazzling smile and he watched me suspiciously for a moment.

'She is just like us, Jed,' Tessa told him, but he turned away and went about his business.

It was agreed that the marriage would take place at noon the next day and as Kane walked with me through the Chapel field, I gave some thought to what I was about to do. I had a brief niggling doubt, but then, looking at Kane's handsome face, I knew that I did not wish to go back on my word. After all, it was I who had urged him not to ask my dear uncle's permission. Surely, I thought, when the marriage was in place, nothing could break it.

* * *

Aggie was in the kitchen when I walked through the door as I sank myself into the chair by the range.

'Whatever ails you?' she asked, concern in her voice. 'You look worn out, Miss Katherine, and I have to warn you that your aunt isn't well pleased that you missed lunch.'

'I am just tired, Aggie, for I have been walking all day and I have had nothing to eat,' I told her.

'Have you been with those gypsies again?' Aggie said, glancing at the closed door before she asked the question.

I had no chance to reply as Aunt Phoebe burst through the door from the hallway.

'Have you lost all your sense of decorum and time, young woman?' she shouted. 'Your hair is loose and looking as if it needs a good brush and your face is burnt from the sun!' My aunt suddenly softened her voice. 'What is wrong with you, child, please tell me? Is it a young man?' At her words, I was tempted to tell her the truth, but I spotted Aggie frowning at me in warning.

'I'm sorry, Aunt Phoebe. I have walked so far,' I explained with a half-truth.

'Get Katherine a bowl of warm water to soak her feet in and a sandwich please, Aggie,' my Aunt instructed and then, looking at me, she continued. 'I suggest that you stay home tomorrow and rest, for you look fair worn out.'

Later that evening, in my room once more, after spending a couple of hours helping Aunt Phoebe mend some sheets while Uncle Zac polished his boots, I set to wondering where I would sleep tomorrow night and rumblings of doubt flickered through my mind again.

As I looked around my familiar

room, my eyes alighted on the keepsake box and I knew I would have to take this with me. I would also need clothes and how could I possibly take it all with me tomorrow? There was only one answer. I would have to come back after the ceremony and enlist Aggie's help.

The thought of the ceremony caused me again to question what I was about to do, but then Kane's gentle arms came into my mind and any doubts I had, vanished. Falling into a blissful slumber, my thoughts were of my love and the beautiful butterfly dance.

4

Late the next morning, I was awakened with a tapping on my bedroom door and as it opened I could see it was Aggie holding a tray laden with tea and toast.

'Good morning, Miss,' Aggie said.

'What time is it?' I asked as the young woman put the tray on my lap and drew back the curtains. As she did so, I could see with some amazement that the sun was already quite high in the sky and I made to remove the tray and its contents, but Aggie stopped me.

'No, Miss, you eat your breakfast and drink your tea while you tell me what is going on,' she said with some authority in her voice.

'What time is it, Aggie?' I repeated.

'It is nine o'clock or thereabouts,' she answered.

'Nine?' I exclaimed. 'I should be

feeding the chickens!'

'Your uncle is doing it,' she told me. 'Now, what is going on? For I know there is something afoot and whatever it is, you can't hold it to yourself, so tell me,' she urged.

I drank the tea and took small bites of toast, mulling over as to what I should tell her and then I made a sudden decision.

'I am to marry today,' I announced.

'Marry!' she exclaimed. 'What do you mean, Miss Katherine?'

'I am to marry a gentleman named Kane today in a gypsy ceremony,' I explained further.

'But, Miss Katherine, you surely cannot do this without the mistress' knowledge!'

'I can and I will, Aggie, for it is what I desire,' I told her honestly.

'Then I'm coming with you. You will need a familiar face for certain,' Aggie offered.

I didn't know what to say.

'But I don't wish to get you in any

trouble, or lose your position here at Northcliffe House.'

'No one will know unless you tell them, Miss, for it is my afternoon off and if we walk together, then your aunt will not be suspicious,' she replied.

'Thank you, Aggie. I accept your offer and I will not breathe a word of your involvement in this,' I assured her.

Aggie left with the tray after we had arranged to leave the house together at eleven thirty, telling Aunt Phoebe we were going for a walk to Monks Cove.

I scrambled out of bed and poured some water from the pitcher into my china wash bowl, the orange flower decoration inside it causing me to think of the butterflies, which strengthened my resolve as I thought of Kane holding me close and whirling me around in the sunlight.

Slipping into my peach blouse that was adorned with white lace and small buttons on the bodice, the thought struck me that I was preparing for my wedding. When the cream-coloured skirt was in place, I then secured an ivory belt around my waist, and then, looking in the mirror at the result, I gasped, for my loose hair made me look every inch a gypsy and not a *gorgio*.

To rectify the matter, I decided to tie my hair back in a knot at the nape of my neck, leaving the top of my hair flat so that the poppy circle, which Maddy was making, would sit comfortably on my head.

Before leaving my room, I looked out of the window at the familiar view I had seen each morning on waking for nigh on twenty years and a tear escaped my eye. Far better, I told myself, that I marry a man I love, than share the rest of my life with someone I felt less for.

I took one last look at the sea and the blue sky, hardly believing that so much had changed for me since the morning of my birthday. As I walked past my dressing table, I took a glance at the keepsake box, which for some reason was very precious to me, vowing to return for it later. I picked up a small brown reticule and placed a lace edged handkerchief in it. At the door, I turned back for one last look, then making my way down the stairs and stepping into the hallway, I could see that the grandfather clock showed the time of quarter to eleven.

'Your aunt and uncle have gone over to Treverrick,' Aggie told me.

'What time do they intend to come home?' I asked, quite alarmed by this piece of information, as I knew that Uncle Zac and Aunt Phoebe may see us walking towards the clearing at the back of the big house.

'About twelve, Miss, so we'd best leave now,' she suggested.

I could see that she was out of cap and apron and wore a delightful blue cotton dress, the material of the skirt falling gracefully to her feet.

'If we are both ready, then your suggestion is a good one,' I agreed with an excited smile.

We made our way swiftly to Monks Cove, for once on the beach, we would not be observed, but on reaching the cove, I could see that the tide was already in, the sea thundering against the rocky coastline beneath us. We both stopped in our tracks.

'The tide! I should have thought of it earlier. We must walk across the cliffs, there is nothing else for it.' I was afraid that my aunt and uncle would see us and my plans would be thwarted, but once safely at the edge of the clearing, I breathed a sigh of relief, sure now that all would be well.

'Who is this?' Jed asked gruffly looking at Aggie, as we stood in front of the caravan.

'She is my maid,' I told him, my voice strong, as I looked him in the eye.

'Maid!' Jed scoffed. 'Once you are wed to our Kane, you will no longer be needing her.'

'I am aware of this,' I responded to his unkind manner, 'but I thought I should have someone of my own to witness my marriage.'

At these words, Kane's father flung

his head back and with hands on hips, laughed uncontrollably.

'What's up, Jed?' Tessa asked as she appeared at the top of the steps.

'Nowt,' her husband answered, walking off towards the stream, a pail in one hand.

'What has amused my husband so?' Tessa asked me.

She looked beautiful today in a full skirt of many colours, with a white lacy blouse, a red belt at her waist, which boasted a silver buckle and a red crocheted shawl across her shoulders. Her hair shone in the sunlight, the black waves cascading down her back, with large gold hoops decorating her ears.

'It would appear he is amused because I wished Aggie to witness the wedding,' I informed her, bringing Aggie, who looked quite bemused by all of this, forward to meet Kane's mother.

'Take no heed of him,' Tessa advised. 'He hasn't a romantic bone in his body that one.'

Maddy appeared with a headdress of poppies. 'Will this do you?' she asked, smiling at her handiwork.

'It is perfect!' I assured her. 'Thank you so much. May I try it on?'

'No, certainly not,' Tessa was very quick to interrupt. 'It is to be placed on to your head just before the ceremony begins. It's a tradition'

'Where is Kane?' I asked, looking around.

'He is in the wagon getting dressed for the occasion,' Maddy told me.

He appeared at the top of the steps and my heart missed a beat at the sight of him. Any doubts I may have had vanished as I looked at him. He was dressed in black breeches with a white open-necked shirt over which he wore a colourful waistcoat.

'So,' Kane began, 'my delightful bride has arrived, thank heaven.'

'I have, indeed,' I responded, my voice quivering with emotion. My whole being was full of love for him and to be united with him in marriage was all I desired.

'And who might this be?' Kane asked, reaching the bottom of the steps and casually encircling my waist with his arm.

'I am Aggie, Sir,' Aggie said. She had been silently watching the scene before her until then.

'Aggie is our maid at Northcliffe and also a good friend of mine,' I explained to Kane. 'She has come to witness our union.'

'Welcome, Aggie!' Kane said in a friendly tone, so different to his father's. 'Now, if we are all ready, let us proceed.'

'Just five minutes,' Maddy interrupted. 'We are still to place the poppy circle on Kate's head.'

'Very well,' he agreed. 'While you do what you have to, I shall gather everyone together.'

With Tessa and Aggie's help, Maddy secured the poppy headdress on my head, fastening it with grips.

'There!' Tessa said. 'Let us have a look at you.'

The three of them stepped back to survey my appearance.

'You look every inch a bride,' Aggie said.

'She does, indeed!' Maddy agreed. 'And the poppies match her blouse perfectly.'

'Are you ready?' Tessa asked.

I could feel myself trembling with anticipation.

'Yes,' I replied nervously.

The three of us walked to the far end of the clearing, Tessa's arm through mine. As we reached the gathering awaiting the marriage ceremony, it was a sight to behold. The men folk all wore colourful waistcoats like Kane and the women, colourful skirts and shawls. In the centre was the bough of yellow, flowering, fragrant broom.

All was silent when I took my place beside Kane. As I reached his side, he took my hand and looked at me with his dark eyes sparkling. I smiled up at him.

'You look captivating,' he whispered.

Jed appealed for everyone to be silent.

'You are both to jump over the flowering broom and then plight your troth to one another in your own words, and all here will witness your giving of one to another.'

Kane looked down at me.

'Are you ready, little one?' he whispered.

'I am,' I told my handsome husband-to-be.

'Lift your skirt up a little!' Tessa called and I did as she suggested. Then, with the one hand in Kane's we jumped over the beautiful yellow broom together.

'I plight my troth to you, Katherine, with love and a promise that I shall care for you the rest of our days. May we be happy and blessed with children. This is my pledge to you.'

Tears sprung to my eyes and then it was my turn. I realised, with some dismay, that I had not given a thought to what I was to say, so I let my heart guide me as I spoke.

'I too, plight my troth to you, Kane, in the presence of all here. My heart will always be full of love for you, as it is today and I pledge myself to you completely, on this our wedding day.' I had almost whispered the words, but knew that every one of them were true.

'Now,' Jed said, 'take this to the stream and collect some water.' He handed a pail to me.

Doing as I was bid, I went to the stream and bent over, placing the bucket in the cool water, which trickled over tiny pebbles and slowly entered the pail. I lifted it out and took it back to the waiting circle of people.

'Pour some into this cup,' Jed instructed. I noticed it was one of Tessa's porcelain cups with the roses on it. Jed took the pail from me.

'Now both drink from the cup,' Tessa called.

The people present, all started to gently clap. We linked our arms, Kane drinking first and then myself, looking into each other's eyes.

Kane suddenly dropped the cup to the ground for I could hear it smash to smithereens beneath us. I was quite alarmed by this, but realised it was part of the marriage ceremony.

'We have exchanged vows to one another and each drunk from the cup of love. Now we are united for ever, as man and wife,' Kane announced as he stroked my cheek with the back of his hand.

'Kiss your wife!' someone shouted and everyone else took up the chant.

Kane smiled at me and tipping my chin upwards, he bent down and kissed me on the lips, his mouth hovering on mine, as gently as a butterfly's wings. I responded to his kiss and everyone yelled 'Congratulations!' in unison. I was somehow separated from my husband, everyone hugging and kissing me, including dear Aggie who had tears running down her cheeks.

'Kane is a very handsome man and a very gentle one,' Aggie whispered to me, her arms around my neck. 'I wish you both happiness.'

Kane took my arm, leading me into the small wood. 'I need to talk to you, little one,' he said, stopping beneath a tree where sunlight filtered through the branches, shining on both of us, which I deemed as a sign of good luck.

'Is there something wrong?' I questioned, suddenly afraid.

'No nothing, I assure you,' he replied, tilting my chin up so I was looking at his face. 'It is just that you will have to go back to your home for a few days while I negotiate for a new *vardo* for us.'

'But I had thought to be with you,' I protested, tears springing to my eyes.

'Do not be upset, Katherine, for I love you. We are now husband and wife and I have your interests at heart. I would not want you to endure sleeping in a tent,' he explained.

'Will it be long?' I asked him, tears starting to trickle down my cheeks. 'For I cannot bear to be without you.'

'It will take but a week or two and then we shall be together, I promise. Now dry your tears,' he said, gently brushing them away with the back of his hand.

'Very well,' I agreed, for what else could I do?

As Kane and I walked back to the clearing hand in hand, I could hear a lively piece of music being played on what must have been a fiddle. As we drew near I could see it was Jed providing the music, and the gathering of my new colourfully-dressed family, including Aggie, were dancing, the women lifting their skirts above the ankles, their feet swiftly moving on the spot in time to the beat. Tessa spotted us.

'Come, Kate, join us,' she said taking my hand and drawing me into the circle.

Watching the others, I gathered my skirt up, my feet starting to keep time to the vibrant music, and I felt at once invigorated, happy and in love all at the same time. The dance came so naturally to me, and as the men folk joined us, we stepped around each other, the men clapping their hands in rhythm with the sound coming from Jed's fiddle. As the music stopped I collapsed, laughing and breathless, into Kane's arms.

'Now for some refreshment,' Tessa suggested.

We all sat in a circle on the ground around the slowly burning fire, Tessa and Maddy handing us all a crystal goblet containing a reddish brown liquid. I could see Aggie on the other side of the circle accept a glass and continue talking to the older couple, laughing at something a handsome man said to her.

I was so happy and then the thought of parting with my husband momentarily marred my good spirits.

'Raise your glasses to Kane and Kate. May they be happy for eternity,' Jed said.

All present lifted their goblets and then drank, Kane and I doing likewise. The pleasant liquid slid smoothly down my throat, warming my whole mouth and lips as I drank.

'What is it?' I asked Kane.

'Dandelion and Burdock wine,' he answered. 'Do you not like it?'

'Of course I like it, Husband, it warms my soul as you do,' I told him.

After a brief interval, in which time Kane and I laughed together and snatched brief kisses amidst our gaiety, we ate food from the cauldron on porcelain plates with silver forks. The concoction of food was delicious and it warmed my whole being.

Suddenly, I felt delightfully sleepy. Leaning against Kane's shoulder, I gently kissed his neck, snuggling up to him as he slipped his arm protectively around me and I felt safe at his very presence, having no doubt in my mind that today I had done the right thing by becoming his wife.

While the other women, Aggie included, washed the dishes in the stream, Kane and I stepped up to Tessa and Jed's *vardo*. As my husband held me close in his arms, me entwining my arms around his strong neck, I looked around at the perfection of the interior of the caravan and could hardly wait for Kane and I to have our own home.

As we stood together for some time, our arms around each other, Kane suddenly moved me away from him, bending towards me, his mouth seeking mine and I knew this was farewell for the time being.

All too soon it was time to go, go back to Northcliffe with Aggie and leave all this behind. But if Kane was true to his word, in a couple of weeks, we would be together for ever. We parted with Kane whispering sweet words of love in my ear and asking me to be patient, but my heart ached at leaving him and I told him so.

'My heart aches, also' he replied, 'but what is a couple of weeks compared to a lifetime?'

I knew his words to be true and I tried to be happy, but as he kissed me farewell, I had an irrational foreboding that our life would not go as Kane and I planned.

Aggie and I left the encampment, turning around every now and then, to see Kane raising his hand in farewell.

'Thank you, dearest Aggie,' I said to her as we approached the whitewashed cottage.

'I enjoyed it, Miss, and I am so pleased I came with you. And Miss,' she whispered as we approached the side door, 'if there is anything I can do for you and Master Kane, please tell me.'

I squeezed her arm and went straight to my bedroom. I had reluctantly removed the circlet of poppies before I left the encampment and given it to Maddy, for she had made it and as I lay on my bed, my head filled with the words Kane and I had spoken that day. It felt as if it was all a beautiful dream and that I was not truly married to him, whom I loved with all my being, but I had to cling to the thought that we would soon be together and I would nestle in his arms again.

With these positive thoughts, I fell into a peaceful slumber, only to be awakened by a commotion downstairs. I could hear someone banging at the front door and Aunt Phoebe's voice calling to Aggie to answer it, but of course, it was Aggie's afternoon off. I quickly jumped off the bed, tidied my hair and smoothed my skirts then made my way to the hall. Aunt Phoebe was already opening the door as I stepped into the hallway.

'Can I help you?' I heard her say.

'I must speak with Kate,' a voice said.

I recognised with some alarm that it was Maddy's.

'There's no Kate here,' Aunt Phoebe told her with indignation as she made to close the door.

I ran towards her and stopped my aunt by catching hold of her arm.

'Katherine, what are you doing?' my aunt asked sharply.

'I think the young woman is asking for me,' I told her.

'She asked for Kate,' my aunt said, 'and you are, always have been and always will be, Katherine!'

'I know, but some do call me Kate outside of the house,' I explained to her.

Aunt Phoebe opened the door wider and I could see Maddy standing there, a shawl draped over her head.

'Kate,' she said urgently, 'you must come at once.'

'Whatever is wrong?' I asked, concern in my voice.

'Your husband has had a fall and he is asking for you,' Maddy said.

Aunt Phoebe's face drained of colour as she looked at me. I tried to catch her as she fainted to the floor.

5

'Fetch the smelling salts, please,' I instructed Aggie as she came into the hallway to see what was amiss. By this time, I had raised Aunt Phoebe's head onto my lap and I could see she was starting to come around. When Aggie arrived with the smelling salts, I passed the bottle to and fro beneath my aunt's nose and after a few seconds, she raised her head and looked at me.

'What shame have you brought on our house, Katherine?' She struggled to her feet.

I realised the front door was still open and Maddy still stood on the doorstep.

'Please come in,' I told her.

'You would ask a gypsy into our home?' my aunt said as she got to her feet and made to close the front door in Maddy's face, but I put a restraining hand on her arm.

'Please, Aunt Phoebe, let the young woman in for she is my sister-in-law,' I implored her.

'I do not understand any of this!' my aunt said, making for the dining room. 'But have it your way and come to me with an explanation after you have seen to this woman.'

Maddy stepped into the hallway and I closed the front door behind her.

'Whatever is wrong with Kane?' I asked her with urgency.

'He fell from the top of the caravan steps and banged his head.'

'Is he badly hurt?' My heart was pounding in my chest.

'He was drunk and probably never felt a thing, but since he came round, he has done nothing but ask for you and was insistent that if I didn't fetch you, he would come here himself.'

I was bemused at Maddy's story, for Kane seemed fine when Aggie and I had left. This thought caused me to think with some alarm, of Aggie and looking around, I could see she had disappeared.

'Why was he drunk?'

'He didn't want you to leave him,' Maddy explained.

'But he insisted I did. If it had been my decision, I would have stayed,' I said emphatically. Now Aunt Phoebe knew of my betrayal and unwilling tears trickled down my cheeks.

'Where are you, Katherine?'

'We must go to her, if you are willing,' I told Maddy.

'I shall come to support you, for it won't be easy,' Maddy perceived.

As we entered the dining room, I could see Aunt Phoebe sitting on the settle, a handkerchief at her nose. I pulled two of the dining chairs out from under the table for Maddy and I to sit on. The whole scene took me back to earlier that day, when Daniel Trevartha had sat on the settle and I wasn't married to Kane. Had it really only been a few hours ago, I asked myself? I noticed Maddy had removed the shawl from her head and had placed it around her shoulders.

'What have you to say for yourself then, Katherine?' she asked, her voice strong once more and authoritative.

'I am in love, Aunt,' I told her, my voice as strong as hers.

'And what does a young woman of your age know of love?' she asked derisively.

'I know what I feel for Kane,' I answered her. 'I felt it the instant I saw him.'

'You talk in riddles, child!' she told me. 'And because of this instant love, you decided to marry him? Was it in front of a priest?'

'No, not in the presence of a priest,' I admitted.

'Thank goodness. If you had, the marriage would be illegal, for you would have needed our permission as you are under the age of twenty-one.'

'But it was a wedding ceremony nonetheless, as real to me and as sacred, as if I had wed in the village

81

church.' By now, I felt my voice rising and realised that I was angry. How could anyone doubt the love Kane and I had for one another? It was as real as the poppies that grew in the meadow.

'So you went against my wishes. I did not want you to associate with that gypsy!' she shouted.

'That is why I didn't tell you,' I told her honestly, 'for fear of what you might say.'

'I'd rather you had told me and I could have put a stop to it, before you married him!' she retorted.

'But I have married him and must go to him for he is asking for me,' I said.

'If you are wed, then why are you still here, Katherine?' she challenged. It was a good question and I had no ready answer for it, but Maddy replied for me.

'Kate is here because my brother, Kane, has to negotiate for a caravan of his own.'

Aunt Phoebe mocked me with a laugh.

'So you are to spend the rest of your life living in a caravan and travelling the country in all weathers? After all we have taught you and for all the care we have bestowed upon you, this is how you treat us? I could weep, Katherine,' she said, rising to her feet.

'May I go now?' I asked.

'No, Katherine, you may not, I forbid it! Now go to your room and until you are over this silly notion. You will not be allowed beyond the gate, on your own' she said, with the usual authority in her voice. 'And be thankful that your uncle is at Treverrick playing cards, for he need never know about this madness, nor anyone else for that matter.'

'You cannot do this!' I pleaded with her, hot tears stinging my eyes and threatening to fall.

'I can do as I please, for I am your guardian and you are under the age of twenty-one. I have a duty to save you from this foolishness, for that is all it is. Now go to your room and I shall show this young woman out, so she can take the news to her brother, that you are to have nothing more to do with him.' Aunt Phoebe took hold of my arm and steered me out of the room and towards the staircase. 'And if your brother,' she said, addressing poor Maddy, 'should attempt to come here, he will be shown no kindness. Tell him to stay away from Katherine and Northcliffe House. He is not welcome here.'

Back in my room, I flung myself on to the bed and sobbed until my heart ached.

A short while later, I heard a key being turned in the lock. Swiftly, I got up from my bed and ran to the door. Turning the doorknob, I shook the door, but to no avail, I was locked in, probably for the night.

There was nothing to do but try to get some sleep and devise a plan for tomorrow. I got ready for bed, thinking all the while of Kane and the loving words he had spoken to me only this afternoon, and before I fell into a restless slumber, I vowed to see him on the morrow.

The next morning came and I realised it would not be as easy as I thought to slip away. On reaching the kitchen for breakfast and taking my place at the table, Aunt Phoebe looked at me sternly.

'You and I are to walk to the village this morning, Katherine.'

My heart sank at her words.

'Very well, Aunt, after I have fed the chickens,' I agreed.

'You are no longer to feed the chickens,' Uncle Zac told me, 'for your Aunt believes that you should be pursuing more feminine pastimes.'

'But I love feeding the chickens,' I protested and looked at Aggie, but she gave nothing away although her eyes were on me all the time.

'No,' Aunt Phoebe said. 'We must groom you for marriage, hopefully it will be to a Trevartha. Daniel is, no doubt, keen on you and your uncle and I would ask that you walk out with him, as he requested yesterday.'

These words were like a dagger in my

heart. Aunt Phoebe seemed very calm about everything this morning and I grasped that she had had all night to work out a plan to keep me away from my beloved. I thought about objecting her suggestion, but stopped, thinking that maybe, to go along with her advice, would, in the long run, give me a better chance of escape.

'Very well,' I told my aunt, 'I will walk out with Daniel, but I can't promise that anything will come of it.'

'Give it time, child,' she said, looking me in the eye, 'for time is needed for love to blossom. I want you to stay in the kitchen with Aggie while I get changed. Then we will go to your room and decide what you are to wear. Come Zac, the hens will be hungry.'

I was thankful when they were gone, for I longed to speak with Aggie.

'Do you see what she is doing to me?' I whispered to her.

'I do, Miss Katherine, and my heart goes out to you, but what can be done? Mistress asked me this morning if I knew of what you were up to yesterday,' the young woman said, with worry in her voice.

'Don't worry, Aggie, I shall say nothing of your involvement, as I promised you,' I told her, 'but I need you to go to Kane and tell him I love him and he must wait until I can free myself from Aunt Phoebe.'

'I will go, Miss, when you are all out and I've done my jobs around the house,' Aggie agreed, 'for I can see how much you and Kane love each other. I wish I could find someone to love me,' she added, dreamily.

'Thank you, Aggie,' I said ecstatic at the thought that she was my link to Kane, who was, no matter what Aunt Phoebe would have me believe, my husband.

* * *

'I knew you would see sense,' Aunt Phoebe said as we looked through my wardrobe for a suitable gown to wear.

'Please don't lock me in again, Aunt,' I pleaded, 'for I promise I will not leave the house at night.'

'Your promises mean little to me anymore, young lady.'

I felt a pang of guilt.

'But I will not lock the door this night if I am sure I can trust you. We will do some sewing this evening, and start to stitch you a nightgown towards your trousseau, for I have a bale of white lawn cotton, which will be perfect. You will not retire early to bed, but go when I do and I shall come in and say goodnight at no given time.'

Her words made me realise how seriously she viewed this predicament I had caused for her and I was aware that there would be no easy escape from Northcliffe House. Not without a chaperone anyway. I suddenly felt a spark of joy at this thought, for surely, in a day or two, my aunt would trust me to walk with Aggie to Monks Cove. Yes, I would work towards this plan. As much as I disliked deceiving my aunt and uncle, my love for Kane was more important than anything I had ever had in my life.

After dinner that evening, I was anxious to see Aggie alone and fervently prayed my uncle and aunt would leave us, if only for a moment. As she served dinner, Aggie kept looking at me and smiling encouragingly, which led me to believe she had met with some success at the encampment. 'May I help Aggie with the dishes, please, Aunt?'

'You may for half an hour while I arrange things for our sewing. It will, at the very least, keep you occupied,' she agreed and I felt myself tremble with anticipation. When alone, I had no need to ask Aggie, she was bursting to tell me.

'I've got a note for you, Miss Katherine, from Kane himself.'

'And how is he after his fall?' I asked anxiously.

'He has a bump on his forehead, but nothing more,' Aggie told me.

'The note, please, Aggie, for I shall

burst if I do not see it.'

Aggie fumbled in her pocket, retrieving the message from Kane.

'Should anyone come in, Miss, hand it back to me the moment you hear the rattle of the door.'

'I will, I will,' I agreed. Aggie pressed the paper in my hand and I noticed that my fingers were shaking. Going over to the window, I unfolded the piece of white paper and read.

Dear wife,

As promised, I shall return for you soon. Be comforted by thoughts of the butterfly dance and dream of only me, as I shall dream of you.

Your Husband,

Kane.

I re-read the words several times, tears dropping from my cheek to my lips, feeling like the gentle touch of Kane's kiss.

'We must hurry or your aunt will return,' Aggie coaxed.

Folding the precious piece of paper, I reluctantly handed it back to her.

'Please place it under my pillow when you have a chance, will you Aggie?' I asked her.

'Yes, Miss, I will for you,' she agreed.

'And Aggie, I'm hoping, no praying, that my aunt will allow me to walk with you in a couple of days, to Monks Cove,' I told her.

'Let us hope so, Miss,' she replied, squeezing my hand.

I spent a couple of days walking with Aunt Phoebe to the village and taking afternoon tea with various genteel ladies, and in the evenings I stitched my new nightgown.

My aunt did not lock my bedroom door again and I did not betray her trust by slipping out of the house in the moonlight, but on the third day, at breakfast, I had to broach the subject of walking with Aggie.

'I have a desire to walk to Monks Cove, Aunt Phoebe, for I miss my daily visit to the beach,' I said quietly.

'You know I cannot allow it,' she firmly replied.

'But surely, if I walked with Aggie as a chaperone, you would have no objection,' I coaxed, after which, there was a pause and I could see my aunt was unsure as to what answer to give.

'I don't see why not, if you have Aggie with you,' she agreed. Such was my joy at her answer that I got to my feet and kissed her on the cheek.

'Thank you,' I told her, suddenly feeling free once more. 'You won't mind, will you, Aggie?'

'No, Miss,' she replied, 'we shall go when I have tidied up.'

Back in my room, I practically danced with delight at the thought of my forthcoming walk with Aggie while feeling a pang of guilt at the same time. But then I thought about how I was being held like a prisoner, when all I wanted to do was be with the man I loved.

I prepared myself carefully for the walk, nothing too elaborate to prevent my aunt from having any suspicions. I dressed in a pink cotton gown, which boasted a panel of small white daisies all around the hem.

Looking in the mirror, I could see, thankfully, that I wasn't overdressed and thought I would wear my small straw bonnet to keep the sun from my cheeks.

I tied my hair back into a knot at the nape of my neck and I was ready. Before leaving my room, I hid the note from Kane in the keepsake box, under the small silver hand mirror, praying it would not be found. Stepping into the hall, I placed the straw bonnet on my head, just as Aunt Phoebe came in from the kitchen.

'You look charming, Katherine,' she complimented me. 'Let us hope you meet Daniel on your walk and by the way, we are invited for dinner at Treverrick tomorrow evening, child.'

My Aunt's words would normally have filled me with a small dread, but today, I was bursting with happiness inside, so I kissed her on the cheek.

'I shall look forward to it, Aunt.'

'There, you are already your old self again, thank the Lord,' she replied, 'and hopefully there will be no more talk of marriage and love, except with a suitable beau.'

Aggie came into the hall and we set off for Monks Cove. As we stepped outside, I went over to Minnie, my faithful pony and gave her a sugar lump. As we walked through the gate, I heard my aunt call from the doorway.

'Please be back in time for lunch, young lady.'

'I will,' I called back to her, raising my hand to wave.

As we reached Monks Cove, I breathed in the sea air and stretched both my arms in the air, for at last, I was free.

'The tide is out, Miss,' Aggie said.

'It is indeed,' I told her with gaiety in my voice as I linked my arm through hers.

We walked along the sand, lingering to throw pebbles into the calm sea as small waves chased each other to the shore. Aggie and I started a game of whose pebble would go furthest out to sea. After much laughter, Aggie won.

'We best go on, Miss Katherine' she suggested.

We walked arm in arm, from the beach toward the encampment, laughing as we went, but our laughter turned to dismay as we caught sight of the clearing. We both stopped in our tracks, looking at each other and both running towards it, stopping at the edge. Tears of frustration ran down my cheeks, for the clearing was empty, apart from a pile of ash from where the fire had burned. No caravans, no colours, no fire and no Kane.

'Don't take on so,' Aggie said, placing her arm around me. 'He said he would return for you.'

'I know,' I sobbed, 'but when? When?' I repeated the word over and over.

'He'll be back for you, you know he will,' Aggie said. 'Think of the note he wrote to you.'

'You're right,' I said, calming down.

'Please walk with me, Aggie, through the meadow.'

'But of course, Miss,' she answered. As we walked through the clearing, all sorts of memories whirled through my mind — brightly painted *vardos*, Kane's laugh, us holding hands as we walked, then, as we passed the spot where we jumped the besom of flowering broom together, I thought of Kane's wedding vows.

'He surely would not desert me, Aggie.'

'No, Miss, he would not, for if I ever saw love on someone's face, it was on his' she assured me.

We walked on through the wood, the sunlight every now and then falling upon us, just as it had that day for Kane and I and as we stepped out of the wood on to the edge of the meadow. My heart ached as I looked at the bright orange poppies swaying gently in the mild summer breeze, and I remembered the headdress that Maddy had fashioned for me.

'It is very lovely,' Aggie commented, 'and I can see now where Maddy got the poppies from.'

We walked along the well trodden path until we reached the top of the incline and I turned back. The view was the same as the other day, the wood, the grey walls of Treverrick, but no gaily painted wagons and my heart lurched with disappointment.

'We should go back,' Aggie urged quietly, 'for if we are late for lunch, Mistress won't let us walk out together again.'

There was sense in the words she spoke, but I needed to walk to the next field.

'Just a little further,' I requested, 'then we will head back.'

At the top of the next field, we could just see the sea in the far distance, a sparkling blue in the morning sunlight. I stopped and Aggie did likewise, then we headed back to the poppy meadow, me thinking all the while of Kane, seeing his white blouson shirt open at the neck, his tanned skin and coal black hair, but above all, his almost black sparkling eyes looking at me.

Just as I thought it, a Red Admiral butterfly flew around me, fluttering slowly round and round, transporting me back to that magical day of the butterfly dance, when Kane had asked me to marry him.

I reached out to the butterfly and it landed fleetingly on my hand and then resumed it's dance around me. I had a curious thought that Kane had sent it to reassure me and amongst the poppies, with the butterfly around us still, I sobbed in Aggie's arms.

6

'Don't look so solemn,' Aunt Phoebe said to me as we were getting prepared to go to Treverrick the next evening. 'You have been quiet all day.'

I looked in the mirror at my violet gown, the skirts of which swirled around me as I moved. Two panels of purple lace had been inserted cleverly in the skirt and the bodice, fashioned to appear as if a short sleeved jacket was worn over it. How I wished I was wearing it for Kane.

'Speak to me Katherine,' Aunt Phoebe urged.

'I cannot go to the big house this evening, or any evening,' I told my aunt. I had been thinking about it all day and at the last minute, I realised that I could not agree to walk with Daniel, for I was a married woman and bound to Kane, in body and spirit.

'I despair of you, child. I take it this is all because of the gypsy Kane, who you would have me believe is your husband,' my Aunt said, the disdain she felt all too apparent in her voice.

'It is because of Kane,' I admitted quietly.

'I wish you to get this nonsense out of your head!'

'I cannot, Aunt. I am sorry, but I love him,' I told her, for what seemed the hundredth time.

'How on earth can you love someone you hardly know? And as for thinking that you are married to him, it is too preposterous for words,' she told me.

'Whatever you say will alter nothing. You very obviously do not understand.' My voice was firm as I spoke.

'Understand?' my Aunt repeated. 'Understand what, exactly? That you are married to a gypsy? After all your uncle and I have taught you about what is right and what is wrong, I cannot believe that you are putting me through this, Katherine.'

'I am sorry,' I began.

'Sorry?' she interrupted. 'If you were sorry, child, this would all be forgotten, but I can see it is not. I am going down to ask your uncle to proceed to Treverrick without us and give apologies for our absence then we are going to have a talk, young lady.'

She left my room and I was on the brink of tears. I will not give her the satisfaction of seeing that I am upset, I thought. I walked over to my dressing table and lifted the lid of the keepsake box, which for some reason calmed me. I would like to have re-read Kane's note, but I knew I didn't have the time, so I slowly shut the lid, just as I heard my aunt call to me.

'Come down, please, Katherine, this minute.'

Knowing there was no escape, I left my room and made my way downstairs to see my aunt standing in the hallway below, waiting for me.

'We will go into the drawing room,' she said unexpectedly, for this room was normally only used for special occasions and Christmas celebrations.

I followed her through the door and shivered on the threshold, for the room was cold and uninviting without a fire burning. Everything was still and unreal, from the settle and armchairs of green-coloured velour, to the large glass-fronted china cabinet which held all my aunt and uncle's treasures.

'Sit down, please Katherine, I am not an ogre,' she said impatiently.

I sat on the edge of one of the armchairs and looked at her. She wore a crimson dress, the skirts boasting a small train. Black velvet ribbon hung in a bow from the bodice and a jacket of the same material finished the outfit off, with short sleeves decorated with white muslin flounces.

Until my birthday, I had looked up to her, but now I realised that she was a very harsh woman and had never showed me any affection. At this moment, I despised her for her total lack of understanding.

'Are you not happy here?'

'You know as well as I, Aunt Phoebe, that I have always been happy here with you and Uncle Zac. I acknowledge that you have always been good to me and given me a good home, but . . . '

'But what, Katherine? Please go on, for I am interested to know how you feel,' my aunt said in her domineering voice, a thing which had never irked me before, but now jangled at my nerves.

'But,' I continued, 'there would have come a time and fairly soon, when I would have married and left Northcliffe to live with my husband. It is the normal way of things.'

'But this, young woman, I'm sure you will agree, is far from normal.' Her voice got louder with each word and she looked at me with eyes of steel.

'Have you ever really loved anyone?' I asked her suddenly, at which question, she looked down at her lap and then raised her head, her gaze steady as she looked at me once more.

'How dare you ask me such a thing, Katherine!' she said, her voice quivering with anger.

'But I must know the answer,' I persisted.

'And what would you gain from such an answer? Tell me, for I am interested to know.'

'I would gain the knowledge as to how you understand my situation,' I said, looking her steadily in the eye. 'For if the answer is yes, then you would know what I feel for Kane, but if the answer is no, then you would have no notion of how I feel at all.'

'This is getting us nowhere,' she pointed out, rising from the chair and going to look at the contents of her glass cabinet.

'I guess, Aunt, that the answer is no,' I dared to say and at my words, her whole body swung around to look at me.

'You go too far, young woman,' she said menacingly.

'I think,' I continued, 'that Uncle Zac

would have more understanding than you.'

'How can you say such things, Katherine? After I have raised you from a babe in my arms. I was a mother to you.' Her voice faltered as she spoke.

'And what of my real mother?' The words slipped out, for we had never before spoken of this topic.

'Your mother, child, was a harlot and a temptress and it would seem you are to take after her!' she said with spite in her voice.

'You hated my mother?'

'I don't wish to talk of it any more, do you understand?' she said, a sob catching her in her throat as she spoke.

'I shall ask Uncle Zac,' I warned her.

'No!' The word was emphatic and there was a fear in her voice, which I had never detected before.

'What are you afraid of, Aunt?' I asked her gently.

'Nothing,' she answered, regaining her composure. 'Go. Go to the man you profess to love.'

'Does this mean that you give Kane and I your blessing?' I asked.

'Certainly not!' she said adamantly. 'I shall never give my blessing on such a union, nor accept it either, till the day I die.'

'I shall go to my room now, Aunt Phoebe, and in a day or two I shall leave Northcliffe, with the hope that one day, you will accept my love for Kane and our marriage,' I said, rising from my seat.

'What sort of marriage do you think you have, child, with no priest and you being brought up to attend church and follow the ways of the righteous? I would have thought that you would find it a travesty as much as I do.'

Her words followed me up the staircase. When I reached my room, I set to thinking that maybe they were true. I sat on my bed for some time, expecting to hear the key turn in the lock of my door, but it did not.

After mulling things over, I decided to seek out Aggie and ask her honest opinion of my marriage at the encampment that day. Thankfully, she was sitting on the chair in the kitchen by the range. 'Whatever is going on, Miss?' she asked as soon as I appeared. 'Mistress has taken to her bed with a headache and I thought you were all going over to Treverrick — you looking so pretty and all.'

'I could not go, Aggie, for my aunt wished me to agree to walk out with Daniel and I cannot. You, of all people, must understand my loyalties lie with Kane.'

'I know, Miss. It is all very difficult for you,' Aggie said truthfully.

'Tell me, Aggie,' I proceeded. 'What do you honestly think of our wedding in the clearing that day?'

'It was beautiful, Miss, and so romantic,' she said dreamily.

'That is so, Aggie, but in all honesty, would you do it?'

'I would if I was to marry someone as handsome as Mr Kane,' she answered getting up from the chair and indicating that I should be seated.

'But it isn't legal, is it Aggie?' I asked, knowing I was asking myself the question as much as I was the young woman.

'Maybe not, Miss, but it is the gypsy way,' she said sensibly.

'But my aunt will not accept it, or give us her blessing. What shall I do, Aggie?' I entreated of her.

'There is a place, Miss,' she began.

'A place? What sort of place?' I interrupted.

'A place where you can get legally married without your guardian's consent, as long as you are over sixteen years,' she told me.

'And where is this place?' I asked, most intrigued.

'It's in Scotland, Miss,' she enlightened me.

'Scotland!' I exclaimed. 'How on earth are we to get to Scotland, if indeed, I can find Kane and also, if he would agree to it?'

'He would, if he truly loves you,'

Aggie said gently, 'and it would give you peace of mind and maybe pacify your Aunt.'

'How do you know this?' I questioned.

'Our Martha and one of the farm hands eloped there when she was seventeen,' Aggie informed me.

'And what did your parents think of this?' I asked the girl.

'They had no reason not to accept it as our Martha and Jim had a piece of paper to prove they was wed,' she told me.

'And where is this place?' I asked, quite intrigued, for if it was a legal marriage, no one, including my aunt, could doubt it.

'If my memory serves me right, it was a village called Gretna Green.'

As she spoke the words, a plan was forming in my mind.

'Thank you, Aggie. All that remains is to find Kane so that I can broach the subject of this village to him and, if as you say, the wedding would be legal, it may solve our problems.' Excitement surged through me at this thought. 'How can I find Kane?'

'He will come back for you,' she assured me. 'One day soon, you will be in his arms again.'

Back in my room after Aggie and I had shared a cup of tea, I settled myself in bed, praying that she was right. Under my pillow lay the note Kane had written to me. I knew the words by heart and recited them I sank into a peaceful slumber.

★ ★ ★

Aunt Phoebe wasn't at breakfast next morning, but dear Uncle Zac was.

'Can I feed the hens today, please?' I asked him, 'I miss it so much.'

'Of course, my dear, while your aunt is indisposed, there will be no harm done,' he agreed.

'Thank you, Uncle.'

How I wished I could tell this dear man what had transpired between Aunt

Phoebe and myself last evening, but then I recalled the fear in my aunt's voice and decided against it. I didn't want to be the one to open old wounds. So, I found myself once more in the sunshine, scattering the corn to the chickens and gazing out to the sea.

Aggie and I walked each day to Monks Cove, but there was no sign of Kane. Every morning we scoured the beach hoping to see him, but to no avail and each day, my spirits sank and I went back to Northcliffe with a heavy heart and little optimism.

'Don't fret, Miss Katherine,' Aggie would say, placing an arm about my shoulder, 'he will come back, for sure.'

So life went on at the cottage. Aunt Phoebe stayed in her room most of the time, instructing Aggie about the household chores and not once, according to Aggie, did my aunt mention me. What Uncle Zac thought of all this I had little idea, for he seemed cheerful enough and still at ease with me.

Two weeks later, Aggie and I made

our way as normal to Monks Cove, when I had a sudden desire to walk on to the clearing.

'Do you think that's wise, Miss?' the young woman cautioned.

'Wise or not, I must go.' Some inner sense told me I should, so we walked, both very hot in the blazing sun, me carrying a pretty parasol decorated with pink flowers.

Eventually we reached the clearing and to my amazement and delight, Tessa's *vardo* was once more standing there, the colours more vivid than I remembered, but all was still and quiet causing me to wonder if it were a figment of my imagination.

'Oh Miss,' murmured Aggie. 'Your instinct was right!'

As we walked towards the caravan, I felt butterflies in my tummy at the thought of seeing Kane once more.

'Tessa,' I called up the steps and miraculously, she appeared in the doorway.

'Kate!' she exclaimed. 'How lovely to

see you. Kane has gone looking for you.' As she spoke, she made her way down the steps and I put my arm around her.

'I'd given up' I told her, 'thinking that you wouldn't come back for me.'

'It is only Kane and I,' she told me. 'He's talked of nothing but you and we had to come back as soon as we could. Now, go on with you and find your husband.' She pushed me gently away from her.

Aggie and I walked back to the beach, me praying all the while that Kane hadn't gone to Northcliffe in search of me and wondering how I was going to broach the subject of Gretna Green to my beloved, but it proved to be an easy task.

We reached the far end of the beach, throwing pebbles and now and then looking to see if Kane was anywhere to be seen, for I was convinced he would walk back to the clearing this way. The tide was starting to come in and Aggie was playing a game of jumping to the seashore and running back before the tiny waves trickled over her shoes, when suddenly she took hold of my arm.

'Look over there, Miss! I'm sure it is your husband.'

I looked in the direction Aggie was pointing to and sure enough, it was Kane, striding towards us. My feet felt rooted to the spot.

'Go to him, Miss,' she urged.

Trembling with excitement, I started to run, each second getting nearer to the man I loved and then I was in his arms and he picked me up, twirling me around and around.

'Stop, Kane. Stop!' I shrieked, laughing all the while, my heart full of warmth now and I realised I should never have doubted him.

'Kate, Kate,' he whispered as he held me close to him. 'How I've longed for this moment.'

'I have, too,' I told him in reply.

'You knew I'd return for you,' he said putting me at arm's length. 'How beautiful you look' and his strong arms encircled me once more. We stood there for some time, me nestling so close to him, I could feel his breath on my cheek.

'Tell me how you've been faring since I've been away from you,' Kane said suddenly.

'Not too well, is the honest answer,' I told him, 'for my aunt will not accept that we are wed.'

'We both knew it would be difficult,' he answered. 'Will you come away with me now?'

'I will, Kane, for I love you, but I need to be at peace with my aunt and uncle,' I told him.

'Then we shall both go and speak with them together?' he suggested.

'No!' I said emphatically, 'for it would be to no avail. Aunt Phoebe even thinks of my dear mother as a harlot, which breaks my heart.'

He sighed.

'Tell me, what would you have us do to resolve this,' he said gently.

'Aggie says there is a place in

Scotland known as Gretna Green where we can marry legally without my guardian's consent. Would you agree to this?' I asked him, my hands on his shoulders as I faced him, looking at his handsome, rugged face.

'Little one, I would do anything to make you happy,' he replied, 'and the sooner the deed is done, the better.'

'But it would take us weeks to get there in the wagon,' I said, my heart sinking, for I wished to resolve this as soon as possible, to enable Kane and I to start our lives together in harmony. As much as I disliked Aunt Phoebe's reaction to all this, I felt I owed it to her and my uncle to do the right thing.

'We will travel up to Scotland as quickly as possible, stopping only a night here and there,' he soothed. 'And once there, we can be married in the correct way to please your aunt and uncle.'

I clapped my hands with glee and called Aggie over to us.

'We are to go to Scotland, Aggie,' I

told the young woman who had been so kind to me.

'That is wonderful news, Miss Katherine,' she said with genuine delight in her voice.

'We must part once more, Kate, but only until tomorrow, when I ask that you come to me and we shall set off on our journey to Gretna Green,' Kane told me, gathering me in his arms once more.

'I hate to leave you,' I told him, planting a kiss on his cheek.

'It will only be for a night, I promise and maybe Aggie will help you with your belongings, if she is agreeable,' he said, looking at the young woman.

'That is all right with me,' Aggie agreed. 'We will come to the caravan tomorrow morning.'

Kane and I said our farewells to each other and as we parted, and I walked along the beach with Aggie, he called out to me.

'Never forget our butterfly dance.'

His words brought tears to my eyes,

as I looked back at his receding figure, I longed to run to him once more, but there were things to be arranged and I knew, that for all our sakes, I must be patient.

That night in bed, all I could see was Kane, a meadow full of orange poppies, Red Admiral butterflies and my husband and I dancing together. With these thoughts, I fell into a contented sleep, longing for tomorrow.

7

The next morning, dressed in my grey dress made of cotton, I sought out my aunt, who I guessed would still be in her bedroom. I needed to see her and talk with her before I left. Reaching her room, I stood for some seconds composing myself then, pulling myself up straight, I tapped gently on the door of her room.

'Come in' she called. Doing as I was bid, I tentatively opened the door.

Aunt Phoebe was sitting in her armchair. The whole room was dark and dreary as the sun had not yet reached this side of the cottage and the heavy, wood furniture made things seem even more gloomy.

'I do not wish to see you, Katherine,' my aunt said as she looked at me with disdain. 'For you remind me too much of your mother.'

'Was my Mother really so terrible?' I asked in a scathing tone.

'She was, indeed. I had no time for her and now, after all you have put me through, I have little, if any, time for you' she told me.

'May I ask you one question?' I said with a strength I didn't feel.

'I will permit one question, Katherine, then you are dismissed.'

'Is my mother dead and did the keepsake box belong to her?' It was something I desperately needed to know and once gone from here, I may never know the answer.

'That is two questions,' she pointed out unkindly. 'Now, which one would you like me to answer?'

I thought for a moment before replying.

'Is my mother dead?' I asked again.

'Yes,' was all she said.

'I am to leave today and start a new life with my husband,' I began. 'Can you see it in your heart to give me your blessing, Aunt Phoebe?'

'No, child, I cannot. Now go, for at least once you are gone, I can come downstairs and I won't have to be reminded . . . '

'Reminded of what?' I asked, tears springing to my eyes. 'You mean my mother, don't you?'

'Please, go, Katherine and never darken our door again.'

At these words, I fled from my aunt's room, the tears which had threatened, falling down my cheeks, and ran headlong into Uncle Zac.

'There, there, child,' he said kindly. 'Whatever has upset you so?'

'It is my aunt,' I told him, sobs catching my throat at each word I spoke.

'Come downstairs with me and we'll get Aggie to make us a strong cup of tea and you can tell me what this is all about.'

His words calmed me and I followed him to the dining room where he left me for a moment to see Aggie. I looked around at everything which was so familiar, thinking of the morning of my birthday and sobs wracked my body once more for how could Aunt Phoebe be so unkind to me and to think she had hated my mother — a mother I'd never known.

I wondered if my mother would have given her blessing to Kane and I and somehow, I instinctively knew the answer to that question was yes. I sat on the settle and Uncle Zac returned. Sitting next to me, he placed an arm around my shoulder.

'Now tell me what all this is about,' he said quietly, as I dabbed at my eyes with a white lace handkerchief.

'I'm in love for the very first time and it's a feeling so strong, I cannot change it or deny it, Uncle Zac,' I told him.

'And why should you change it, or indeed, deny it?' he asked kindly.

'Uncle, I have married the object of my affection and Aunt Phoebe will not give us her blessing.'

My Uncle sat back and leant his head against the back of the settle.

'Who have you married, child, for I know nothing of this?'

'It is Kane O'Brien. He is a gypsy.'

The colour drained from my uncle's face and all was quiet for several moments. I was just about to speak, when Aggie bustled in with the tea, depositing the tray on the table. She looked at me with troubled eyes.

'Would you like me to pour these for you, Miss Katherine?'

'Thank you, Aggie, but I shall do it,' I told her as I got up and walked across to the table and poured the tea into two china cups. I walked over to him and handed him the cup and saucer. I noticed his colour had returned and looking at him, I was suddenly taken back ten years when my dear uncle had been a good-looking man of slimmer proportions.

'Are you alright, Uncle?' I asked him, concern in my voice, for I could tell that my news had affected him deeply.

'You words came as a shock, Katherine, that is all. Let us drink the tea and then we will talk,' he said.

'You won't berate me as Aunt Phoebe did, will you?' I pleaded with him and he laid a hand across one of mine.

'No, child, I shan't berate you, have no fear,' he said quietly and finished his tea. He placed the cup and saucer on the table before us. 'I take it this was a marriage of the gypsy kind?'

'It was, indeed, Uncle. Please, tell me that I have your blessing' I beseeched earnestly of him.

'First of all, tell me what your aunt has said to upset you so.'

'She said my mother is a harlot and a temptress and I am the same. She doesn't wish me to darken your door again,' I told Uncle Zac quietly. My uncle once more placed his arm around my shoulder.

'Your mother was a sweet, kind person and you are very much like her. Take no notice of your aunt's comments. Things have a habit of returning to haunt us as we get older.'

Although I didn't quite understand

what Uncle Zac had said, the fact that he had claimed my mother had been sweet and kind was enough for me.

'Have you ever loved, Uncle?' I asked him and he was quiet for several moments with a thoughtful, faraway expression on his face.

'Yes, I have loved Katherine, very deeply in fact,' he said gently.

'So you understand how I feel?' I asked, with anticipation of his answer.

'I understand completely.'

I hugged him.

'So you will give us your blessing?' I asked, looking at his dear face.

'I give you both my blessing,' he agreed and tears of joy started to fall. I could leave Northcliffe today with a happy heart.

'I am to leave today, Uncle,' I told him.

'Then I shall come with you to see you on your way, my dear,' he replied. 'But I shall miss you for you are the light of my life and I shall look forward to your visits.'

'But Aunt Phoebe will not welcome us here,' I said sadly.

'She will, given time, child, I promise you,' he told me and I knew his words were to pacify me and send me on my journey with a smile.

We both rose from the settle and I had a sudden thought.

'Tell me, Uncle, did the keepsake box you gave me on my birthday, belong to my mother?' I asked him.

'Yes,' he said, turning me towards him. 'Treasure it always, Katherine, for it is all you will ever have of her. Now, let us get you on your way with the man you love.'

My heart sang at Uncle Zac's words and I sped up to my room to gather some things together in my portmanteau. I knew I could not take all my clothes, but I neatly folded most things I would need, including the cream skirt and orange blouse I had worn to wed Kane, for I would wear it at Gretna Green. Then, I wondered if we would have to renew our wedding vows, as my uncle had given his blessing after all, but I dearly wished for Aunt Phoebe's consent, too.

The last thing I packed with my clothes, was the precious keepsake box, all the more precious now that I knew it had belonged to my mother and as I lifted it down and held it in my hands, I thought how a mother I had never known or been able to love, had held this exquisite box.

I found some tissue paper and wrapped the precious box carefully, before placing it amongst my clothes and then I was ready to start a journey with my husband.

I took one last look around my room then looked from the window once more at the view before me. The sun was now high in the sky, sending sparkling jewels scudding across the water and then I thought of Minnie. I could not leave Minnie behind. Quickly, I picked up the portmanteau and hurried from the room to seek out Uncle Zac and say farewell to Aggie.

'Uncle Zac,' I said, finding him in the kitchen, 'what will I do about Minnie?'

'Don't fret, Katherine, I shall take her over to Treverrick, to the stables there, and when you are camped here, you can ride her, as Kane does his horse, Thunder,' he told me.

At his words, I realised that I had quite forgotten about Thunder. I turned to Aggie who was peeling potatoes at the sink.

'Dear Aggie,' I said to her as I hugged her, 'Uncle Zac is coming with me so I will not need your help today, thank you.'

'I know, Miss,' she said sadly.

'But come along if you wish,' I told her, seeing how upset she looked. 'That will be all right, Uncle, won't it?' I asked him.

'Indeed,' he said. 'I will put it right with your aunt when we get back.'

Aggie smiled once more and untying her apron, slipped it over her head and placed it on a chair.

'Well, let us go, child,' Uncle Zac

urged me as he headed for the back door.

'No, Uncle, I wish to leave by the front door, please.'

'As you wish, Katherine,' he agreed amiably, picking up my portmanteau. As we walked through the hallway, I looked up the stairs with some vain hope that Aunt Phoebe would appear to wish me well, but the staircase was empty and still.

As I passed the grandfather clock, it started to chime the hour of ten, as if in farewell. I passed the dining room door where so much had happened of recent days and then I was stepping through the front door, for what I thought would be the last time.

I fussed Minnie and told her I would see her soon and then followed Uncle Zac and Aggie out of the gate. Glancing back at the cottage, I saw movement in an upstairs window and I knew it was my aunt watching me go. At least she had bothered to look, I thought, which cheered me somewhat and then without another look back, I proceeded to the clearing, with Uncle Zac carrying my baggage and Aggie's arm through mine.

We had to walk over the cliffs as the tide was already in at Monks Cove and when we were half way across, I could see a figure striding towards us, in the distance. Realising it was Kane, I picked up my skirts and ran towards him, as he quickened his steps and ran towards me and at last, his arms were around me and I knew we would never be apart again.

'I thought you weren't coming,' he whispered as he stroked my hair.

'I have good news,' I said. 'My dear uncle has given us his blessing.' As I spoke, Uncle Zac and Aggie caught up with us.

'Thank you, Zachariah!' Kane said, putting me gently from him.

'You know each other!' I exclaimed.

'We have met at Treverrick on a few occasions,' Uncle Zac told me, 'and I know that Kane is a very good man. He will take care of you.'

'You have no qualms regarding my status in life?' Kane asked.

'None,' my uncle replied.

We walked on and my husband and uncle talked and so did Aggie and I.

'You will not get into any trouble when you go back' I said to Aggie, stopping for a moment. 'My uncle will ensure that all will be well, I promise you.'

'I shall miss you, Miss Katherine,' Aggie told me.

'And I, you,' I answered honestly, 'I thank you for all your loyalty.'

'Come, Miss, let's be happy, for we will see each other again before too long and I hope all goes well at Gretna Green.'

Our farewells said, we had to run to catch up with the men folk who had nearly reached the clearing. I could see that the wagon was ready to go, with the horse already harnessed to the *vardo*.

'I will leave you here, Katherine,' my uncle told me. 'Kane tells me you are to go to Gretna Green to marry our way, but I have told him I will give my consent to your marriage here if it will spare you a long journey.'

'Thank you, Uncle Zac,' I said as I put my arms around him.

'We will talk about what is best to do.'

Kane's words drifted across to me and I released my dear Uncle.

'If we did marry here, would my aunt accept this, do you think?'

'When I return home, I will talk to your aunt' he promised me, 'but I can't say what her answer will be — she is a very stubborn woman, as you well know.'

'I'm sure, Uncle, that you will do your best.'

'In view of the new circumstances and our need to talk, little one, we will stop here for the night,' Kane suggested, 'and on the morrow, we will come to see you at Northcliffe, Zachariah.'

'And I shall welcome you,' Uncle Zac

agreed, 'but unfortunately, I can't speak for my wife' he said sadly.

'Until tomorrow then, Uncle,' I said kissing him and Aggie, both on the cheek. I watched as they walked towards the cliff path, feeling uncertain about everything except Kane's love for me and mine for him.

Tessa welcomed me and agreed to spend a further night in the clearing, when Kane explained what Uncle Zac was prepared to do.

'You know it will mean marrying in a church,' Kane's mother told him.

'I do, Mother, but I am prepared to do whatever is possible to make Kate completely happy,' Kane told her.

'I don't know what your father will say, but I am agreeable to anything which makes you both happy,' she said hugging us both. 'Now while Kane unharnesses Monty, we will light a fire, for we shall need to eat later,' Tessa suggested.

Tessa and I collected wood for a fire which we got going, while Kane unharnessed the horse. I learned that underneath the wagon there was a large cupboard known as the 'pan box', which was like a larder and held the provisions. Tessa and I fetched out some vegetables to prepare for the cauldron and I could see that the larder already held bread, tea, coffee and various items. I found this all very interesting and knew I had a lot to learn about the Romany way of life, but I also knew that I would love it.

After we had put the cauldron over the fire and the horse was grazing on the grass behind the *vardo*, Tessa suggested we unpack my portmanteau.

'Come,' she said to me and I followed her up the familiar steps into the wagon. Undoing my baggage, I first lifted out the keepsake box, gently unwrapping the white tissue paper.

'That is beautiful!' Tessa exclaimed with incredulity in her voice. 'Where did you get it, Kate?' she asked with interest.

'My aunt and uncle gave it to me on

my birthday,' I told her. 'My uncle said it belonged to my mother.'

'May I look at it, please?' Tessa asked. I carefully passed the precious box to her and she sat on the locker seat, gazing at it. 'May I open the lid?'

'Of course you may,' I agreed, for I could see that Tessa was as enraptured as I was with it.

She opened the lid gently and examined the contents, a lone tear trickling down her cheek.

'I'm sorry,' she said, wiping the tear from her cheek, 'but I love beautiful objects and this is exquisite,' she told me, saying the same word I had to describe the keepsake box which I was very proud to own. 'Well, let us get your clothes in the chest of drawers,' she said suddenly, handing the box back to me. 'We will store this safely in the chest of drawers also.'

My clothes and the keepsake box put safely away, Kane suggested that we walk to the meadow so we could talk of our future. I agreed with joy in my heart, for I longed to be alone with him.

Holding hands, we walked through the small wood where birds sang from the trees and as we stepped into the meadow, the sight of the poppies still swaying in the breeze, brought back to me our butterfly dance and our gypsy wedding which was so sacred to me that I didn't really wish for another. As far as I was concerned, that day in the clearing, when we had jumped the broom and made our troth to one another, was the most lovely way of marrying that I could possibly imagine.

'You are thoughtful, little one,' Kane observed, stopping on the path we walked between the poppies.

'I'm thinking, that if I had my way, our wedding would be the only one we would have,' I confessed to him.

'But we need to please your family, Kate, do we not?' he said sensibly.

'I guess we do,' I said, quite downcast at the thought, for all I wished was to be a proper wife to my gentle husband.

'I wish to lie with you at night and

not walk with you in my dreams,' Kane said turning me to him, 'and if it means peace of mind for me as much as you, then I'm prepared to wed your way.'

'You are so understanding, Kane, it is no wonder I love you so.'

'Then what are we to do, little one? Is it Scotland or here?' he asked, giving me the choice.

'Here,' I said, making a sudden decision, 'for although we have the banns to call for three weeks, it will be quicker than travelling to Scotland and arranging it there. Perhaps my aunt may condescend to join us and see us united with her own eyes. I can but hope.'

'Then that is what we shall do,' he told me, bending to kiss my lips just as a butterfly flew around us.

I knew it was a good omen and I had hopefully made the right decision.

That night, as I lay next to Tessa on the top bed in the wagon, listening to an owl hooting somewhere in the woods, with Kane asleep in his tent outside, I mulled over what else could thwart Kane and I in our quest for happiness. At least, lying at last between the lovely white sheets with the crocheted edging gave me some comfort.

8

The next morning, I awoke to the sound of birds singing in the trees and I recognised the blackbird's song in particular, sweet, pure and a joy to listen to. Tessa no longer lay beside me and the curtains were still pulled to prevent the morning light seeping into the wagon. I lay for a while, listening to the blackbird's song, hardly believing that I had at last spent a night in the *vardo*.

Negotiating myself from the top bed, I looked at the bottom one and could see what Tessa had meant yesterday. It was not as long as the one I had slept in and was only suitable for a child. I mused as to whether Kane had slept in it as a child.

Dressing myself in a turquoise-coloured cotton skirt and white short-sleeved blouse, I opened the door of the *vardo* and made my way down the steps. Kane and Tessa were sitting in the clearing eating bread and butter. Kane rose to his feet when he saw me.

'Good morning, Kate,' he greeted me coming across and kissing my cheek. 'Did you sleep well?'

'I haven't slept so well since I met you,' I replied laughing, as I looked at his handsome face.

'I will get you a towel,' Tessa called, 'for you will need to freshen up.'

I washed in the stream, taking note of the cool water running on its way across small boulders. What an idyllic scene, I thought as I dried myself with the towel Tessa had supplied me with.

I felt so happy and free that I could have danced on the spot, but I refrained from doing so as Kane called me over to take some breakfast with them. Tessa indicated for me to sit by her on the grass as she handed me a plate and I set to eating the bread and butter, realising I felt quite hungry.

'Tell me about your family, Kate,' Tessa said.

'I'm afraid there is little to tell,' I replied.

'Well, tell me what has happened to you in these past twenty years,' she persisted.

'I never knew my mother,' I began, 'nor know who she was or where she came from. In fact, we've never spoken of her until this past week.'

'So you have no idea who she was?' Kane asked.

'None,' I responded. 'All I know is that Uncle Zac and Aunt Phoebe raised me from a babe in to the young woman you see before you now.'

'And have you been happy, Kate?' Tessa enquired.

'Yes, I have, although the past year I have felt restless and wished for some excitement and purpose in my life,' I said.

'And now you have found it.' Kane laughed.

'I have, indeed, and it is all I could

have wished for.'

Our eyes locked together for some seconds.

'Are your aunt and uncle your true kin? Were they related to your mother or your father?' Tessa asked.

'My father,' I replied quietly. 'I have never given any thought to my father really.' As I spoke the words, I realised it was true — I had never once, until this moment, questioned as to who my father may be.

'So do you think you are related to the couple who you call aunt and uncle?' Tessa said.

'Do you know, Tessa, I have no idea at all,' I told her, turning to look at this lovely woman who I felt I had known all my life.

She laid a gentle hand on my arm.

'And have you always lived at Northcliffe?' Kane asked.

'For as far back as I can remember, yes,' I replied. 'Except for the time I spent at the Academy For Young Ladies in Truro.'

'Why were you there?' Tessa asked.

'The truthful answer is, my aunt wished me to marry well and was always hoping I would marry one of the Trevartha family,' I answered.

'So you have thwarted her plans,' my husband observed.

'I suppose I have.' I gave a little laugh. 'Thankfully, you walked my way and I no longer have a dread of etiquette and grand dinner parties and living at Treverrick — a place I dislike immensely.'

'You are here now and that is all I could wish for,' Kane told me intently. 'Now let us drink more coffee and then we must make our way to see your uncle and aunt if that is possible.'

'I dread the thought of it,' I told him honestly, thinking of Aunt Phoebe's hostility to me only yesterday. 'I very much doubt that my aunt will see either of us,' I warned him.

'You will have me by your side, so have no fear, little one,' Kane reassured me.

'May I help you with anything?' I asked Tessa.

'No, you two young people go and arrange your marriage, for the sooner the better'

'I just have to feed Monty first,' Kane said.

'May I go on ahead across Monks Cove, please?' I asked him.

'You love it there, don't you?' my husband observed.

'It is the tranquillity I love and the sound of the waves lapping on the beach,' I told him.

'You go on ahead,' he told me. 'And don't look so worried.'

* * *

I walked happily to Monks Cove on my own and once on the beach, throwing pebbles in the water, I set to thinking of all that had happened in recent days. Had I really been wilful and gone against all that my aunt had wished for me? My dear Uncle understood as I expected he would, but my aunt was hard-hearted.

Kane made me jump by placing his hands gently on my shoulders. He held me closely in his arms, kissing my loose waves of hair.

Alarmed at this thought, I withdrew from Kane's embrace.

'What is the matter?' he said with worry in his voice.

'My hair,' I uttered, 'I haven't tied it back!'

'And nor should you,' he told me gently, 'for it is part of your beauty.'

'But my aunt will be aghast that I am wandering around the bay with loose hair for all to see,' I explained.

'It will be fine,' he assured me, but as we walked towards Northcliffe, my thought was that Kane had never before been on the receiving end of my aunt's wrath.

The first thing I noticed as we approached the cottage, was that Minnie was gone and I pacified myself at the thought that she was being well cared for at Treverrick.

Approaching the front door, I felt myself trembling, recalling Aunt Phoebe's words — 'never darken our door again'. But my Uncle had agreed to us coming and, after all, it was his home as much as it was hers. Kane lifted the heavy brass knocker, the sound of which would now be reverberating through the hallway and up the stairs. It suddenly seemed a lifetime since I had left here yesterday. The door opened slightly and I could see it was my aunt who peered out at us.

'Aunt Phoebe, we have come to see you and Uncle Zac,' I said meekly as she opened the door a little wider.

'I told you yesterday never to darken our door again with your presence!' she said harshly and I turned to look at Kane.

'Did Zachariah tell you of our plan to marry in the church here?' Kane asked politely.

'He did,' she answered, 'but I still do not hold with it and if my husband is to be foolish enough to give his consent, then so be it, but do not expect me to go along with it and that is all I have to say to you. Good day!' She was about to close the door, but thankfully, at that moment, Uncle Zac appeared behind her.

'No, Phoebe,' he said forcefully, taking hold of the door and pulling it open wider.

'How could you, Zachariah?' she bemoaned. 'After us being married all these years and this is how you treat me. I wonder what Katherine would think if only she knew the truth!'

'What does Aunt Phoebe mean by that?' I asked, quite perplexed.

'It is nothing, child,' my uncle assured me. 'Now leave this to me,' he said, stepping out of the front door and closing it behind him.

'What did Aunt Phoebe mean?' I asked him again.

'Nothing, Katherine, it's just a notion she has. Now let us forget it and go to the church to see Parson Greenaway,' he suggested in his normal kindly manner.

I had never before known my uncle to speak in such a manner to Aunt Phoebe.

'Do you think your wife will accept my marriage to Katherine one day?' Kane asked Uncle Zac, as we walked across the cliffs to the lovely little church that had been built overlooking the sea and a small beach covered with golden sand.

'She will, you have my word on that,' my uncle told Kane and then we strolled in silence.

As we walked down the lane that led to the church, I stopped and so did my husband and uncle for it was a truly glorious sight to behold — the small, grey, stone church with its squat tower and a backdrop of sea and sand.

As we stood looking at the scene before us, I could hear 'the waves crashing lightly to the shore and see the seagulls circling above.

'What a delightful place,' Kane acknowledged.

'It is,' agreed Uncle Zac. 'Now let us hope the Parson is here.'

We made our way along the narrow path which led to the main church door. Uncle Zac opened the door and stood to one side for Kane and I to enter. As we stepped on to the flagstone floor and Uncle Zac closed the door behind him, it took some minutes for our eyes to adjust to the darkness.

'This is the first time I have stepped into a house of God,' Kane whispered to me and I could tell by his manner that he was quite in awe of it as we walked down the aisle to the Vestry, in search of Parson Greenaway.

We were in luck as he was there, donning his vestments. He looked up from what he was doing.

'Good day to you, Mr Johnson and Miss Johnson and you Sir, welcome to our church,' he said. 'How can I help?'

'Katherine and Kane wish to marry, Parson, and I am here to give my consent, as Katherine is only twenty years of age.'

'I thought it may be a wedding when I saw the young couple,' the Parson beamed. He was a slender, kindly man of about forty-five years, with blonde hair, curling at the nape of his neck.

'And when had you hoped to marry?' enquired the Parson, going over to his small desk in one corner of the Vestry, and reaching for a large book which was obviously a diary of church business.

'In three weeks, if possible, Parson,' I said quickly. He turned and raised an eyebrow, looking at my stomach. 'Oh no,' I protested, realising what he was thinking and feeling quite embarrassed at the thought.

'We wish to marry soon, to enable us to travel,' Kane explained to the perplexed looking Parson.

'Travel,' he said. 'Are you a military man, then?' he asked with interest.

'No. Kane is a gypsy,' I said without any thought.

'A gypsy,' he reiterated, his eyebrow raised even higher. 'I'm sorry. I don't know how I stand with this request,' he said, shutting his diary with a flourish.

'Please, Parson. There is no harm in it and Katherine is a good Christian girl, as you know, and these lovely young people are in love,' my uncle pleaded.

'I have no doubt they are and a fine couple they make,' he said understandingly, 'but I don't know how I stand on marrying someone who is not of the Christian faith,' he explained.

'Won't my faith do for the both of us?' I said, stepping forward. 'Could you at least read the banns while you find out how you stand?' I suggested, desperately wishing this to be resolved.

'Well, I could, Miss Johnson, as I know you and your uncle so well,' he agreed, 'but I would ask that both you and Kane attend the reading of the banns each Sunday morning for three consecutive weeks.'

'Thank you, Parson,' I said with relief.

If he hadn't agreed, this would have

been yet another obstacle to overcome.

'I will be able to pencil in a tentative Service of Marriage for you for June the fourteenth, if that is acceptable?'

'It is, indeed,' Uncle Zac said with joy.

'I will require you to sign a consent form, Mr Johnson, please, and I wish these young people to take away this prayer book with the Marriage Service in it and read it fully,' he instructed.

'Indeed we will, Parson,' Kane agreed.

'And where are you both residing?' the Parson's asked.

Kane and I looked at each other, wondering if this was another complication.

'In the clearing behind Treverrick,' Kane bravely told him.

'Both of you?' he questioned, raising his eyebrow once more.

'Yes, Sir,' I said honestly.

'This won't do. No, indeed, it will not,' he said. 'First of all, let me speak to Mr . . . ?'

'Kane O'Brien,' my husband obliged.

I wondered how high Parson Green-away's eyebrow would rise if he knew we had already jumped the broom.

'And how long have you resided in the, eh, clearing?'

'Four weeks,' Kane answered.

'Well, that is at least in order. Now, Miss Johnson, tell me, why you are not living at home?' he asked of me.

'It is only one night she has spent in the wagon — with her intended's mother, I hasten to add. She will be coming back home today,' Uncle Zac argued.

'A little holiday,' the Parson murmured. 'Well, that I can understand. So I shall see you all in church on Sunday morning, then?'

We all nodded in agreement.

'Thank you,' I said to the Parson as we left. 'We really do love each other and wish to do the right thing.'

'I'm sure you do, young lady,' he murmured.

I was thankful when we stepped back

out into the sunlight. As we walked back down the church path, my step was light for I knew that in three weeks, Kane and I would be able to start our journey together in earnest.

'I thought you meant it, Uncle, when you said I would be coming back home today,' I said.

'I do mean it, child. Until the ceremony, you are to come back home with your aunt and I.'

'But Uncle Zac, my aunt will not allow it and she will make my life so unpleasant I will have to leave again,' I protested.

'Katherine,' he said, stopping and taking my hand. 'You are to do the right thing and come home. Your aunt will think more of it than if you were to stay with Kane and his mother in the wagon. Think about what I say.'

'Your Uncle is right,' Kane agreed. 'If you want your aunt's blessing, then this is the best course to take.'

'Very well,' I told them both, 'but if

Aunt Phoebe is rotten to me, then I shall leave.'

'Don't be a defeatist, child. We have to coax your aunt round to our way of thinking and this is the best thing to do. If you and Kane truly love one another, then you can wait another three weeks to be together.'

'But I can see Kane, can't I?' I asked with alarm.

'Of course you can,' my Uncle agreed. 'You won't be a prisoner, I assure you.'

'There. All is sorted,' Kane said happily, taking my hand.

As we walked back to the clearing and the wagon to collect my possessions, all I could think of was that Kane and I were to be parted again. I prayed Aunt Phoebe would agree to my going home. Her words — 'How would she feel if she knew the truth?' — were imprinted in my mind as I returned to Northcliffe

9

Uncle Zac and I went into Northcliffe through the back door. My heart missed a beat when I saw Aunt Phoebe making pastry with Aggie.

'Miss Katherine!' Aggie exclaimed.

Aunt Phoebe looked up and saw us standing there.

'Zachariah,' she said with her usual forceful tone. 'Why have you brought Katherine back with you, knowing how I feel?' She crossed to the sink to wash her hands.

'Katherine is to stay here in her home until she marries Kane O'Brien,' my uncle told his wife in a firm tone as he placed my portmanteau on the floor and put a protective arm around me.

'I will not have the child in this house, Zachariah,' Aunt Phoebe said, wiping her hands. 'Now please go, Katherine.'

'She will not go!' Uncle Zac protested with an authority in his voice that I had never heard before.

I could see my aunt was taken aback by his tone.

'Very well,' she condescended, 'if that is to be, the child can stay in her room.'

'She will not stay in her room!' said my Uncle indignantly. 'She will eat with us and feed the chickens and come and go as she always has.'

How grateful I was for my dear Uncle's words.

'As you say,' she conceded, realising that her husband would broach no argument. 'But do not expect me to be civil, or indulge in conversation with her.'

'How childish you are, Phoebe!' my uncle told her. 'And all because the dear child has fallen in love with a man who you don't approve of, even though you do not know him.'

'I do not wish to know him, for he is a gypsy.'

'You will be civil to him and attend

church with the three of us to hear the banns read, starting tomorrow,' Uncle Zac told her, 'and you will be pleasant to this dear child, who has committed no sin.'

'A thing you would know all about,' my aunt retorted.

'Yes, indeed, a thing I would know all about,' Uncle Zac admitted.

'Are you going to tell this child the truth about her birth?'

'I will do so when the time is right,' my Uncle promised.

'I would dearly love to know,' I said pleadingly.

'You will know, Katherine, I promise you, but not today,' my Uncle told me gently. 'Now, let us take your belongings to your room and maybe Aggie will help you unpack.'

'A pleasure, Miss Katherine,' Aggie agreed. She had watched the scene before her with wide-eyed interest.

I found myself back in my room again, with Aggie helping me hang my clothes once more.

'It is good to have you back, Miss,' Aggie said kindly. 'Are you to marry Mr Kane in the church, then?' she asked.

'It would seem so, Aggie, for propriety's sake,' I told her, 'but if I had my way, my wedding in the clearing behind Treverrick would suffice.'

'That were a lovely day,' Aggie said dreamily, going over to look from the window. 'There's cloud bubbling up, Miss, looks like we could have some rain.'

Indeed, it did rain that night, the gale from the sea causing the raindrops to lash at my window pane as I lay in bed, thinking the weather matched my mood and the misery I felt at being parted from my beloved once more.

The next morning, the sun shone again, but small clouds scudded across the sky and puddles of water lay on the ground. Aunt Phoebe breakfasted with us, but true to her promise, she did not speak until she finished eating.

'I have found three pairs of sheets for you to repair, Katherine, which should keep you out of mischief. I have laid them on your bed.' She rose from her chair. 'I am now going to get ready for church and I expect you to do the same, child. Let us go along with this charade for as long as it takes, for I feel it will come to nothing.'

As she reached the door, she turned back to me.

'Have you lain beside this Kane?'

'I promise you I have not, Aunt,' I replied civilly.

'Then we must thank the Lord for that,' she retorted, sweeping from the room.

The four of us walked across the cliff to the church, my aunt, uncle, Aggie and myself. I linked my arm through Uncle Zac's, and trembled with anticipation at seeing Kane.

The view beyond the church was grey and frothy brown waves tumbled after each other to the shore. I shivered, hoping that the change in the weather was not a bad omen.

We sat in a pew awaiting the start of

the service. The Trevartha family, with Constance's sister, Patience, sat on the other side of the church in the family pew and Daniel kept looking across at me and smiling, but I had no interest in him. Where was Kane? Turning around every now and then, I could see no sign of him.

'Sit still, Katherine. Think of what you have been taught,' Aunt Phoebe told me.

The organ started to play the notes to 'Rock of Ages' when I heard the latch on the church door rattle. I turned around to see Kane and his mother step into the aisle and take a seat. Several other people looked, too, and then we started to sing the hymn. I stumbled over the words, as all I could think of was Kane. He looked so handsome in a white shirt and black jacket, his unruly black wavy hair smoothed back to look tidy.

I hardly took notice of the sermon being read, but I was filled with joy as the Parson read out our names — Kane

O'Brien and Katherine Johnson. The service was over and I was restless to get out of the church and speak to Kane, but my Aunt held me back with a firm pressure on my arm. How I wished to struggle free, but I thought of Uncle Zac's words and I kept hold of my temper.

Once outside in the sunshine, there was no sight of either Kane or his mother and my heart sank.

'Be patient, child,' my Uncle whispered and I heeded his words.

Once back at the gate of Northcliffe, I could not hold back my anxiety to see Kane.

'I am going for a walk,' I told the three of them and before anyone could argue, I set off for Monks Cove.

'You have your Sunday best on,' my aunt called after me with anger in her voice and I looked down at my royal blue gown and jacket made of fine silk. I almost went back to change, but I decided against it knowing that I could be in a lot of trouble when I finally returned to Northcliffe.

The tide was in at Monks Cove, the waves crashing on the rocks of the cliff. I removed my bonnet, untying the ribbon and then loosening my hair from its pins and I suddenly felt as free as a bird again. Reaching the clearing, I could see Tessa sitting on the steps of the *vardo*. Then I spotted another *vardo* brightly-painted and looking like new. I picked up my skirts and ran. Kane appeared from behind the newer wagon, catching me in his arms as I flew towards him.

'A surprise for you little one!' he said, kissing my hair.

'Is it ours?' I asked breathlessly.

'It is, indeed. My father has brought it from Dorset as we arranged.'

He released me from his embrace and I ran to the front of the *vardo* and could see it was of the barrel type, with high wheels and a stable door as Tessa's had. The colours of red and yellow were magnificent. I could see that 'K' and 'K' had been entwined together on one side of the stable door.

'It is beautiful,' I enthused, 'and it is really ours?'

'It is Kate,' he said proudly. 'This is where we will live, love and laugh for the rest of our lives.'

'Can I go inside?' I asked excitedly.

'But of course, little one, it is yours as well as mine.'

We climbed the steps together and I surveyed the beautiful interior. Even the barrelled ceiling had been painted in reds and yellows to match the exterior. It was delightful! There were two beds, one above the other across the back and someone had already made the top one up with the white sheets and the crocheted edging peeping out from under the blanket. There was a stove and a china cabinet, a chest of drawers and a locker seat, all beautifully upholstered.

'Oh, Kane!' I said, putting my arms around him. 'It is lovely and I can hardly wait to travel in it and sleep in it with you.'

'We will be happy, I promise you,' Kane said softly.

'But we must ... ' Kane began, putting me from him, 'adhere to your uncle's wishes.'

'I know,' I agreed, 'but my aunt still thinks that we will end and very soon.'

'Never!' Kane shouted. 'Never, Kate, for now that I've found you, I will never let you go.'

We stepped out into the clearing and I acknowledged Jed.

'Are you pleased with your *vardo*, Kate?' he asked

'I am, Jed,' I told him, as he went on his way searching for wood for the fire.

'Why did you leave the church so quickly?' I asked Kane.

'Because I didn't want to incur your aunt's wrath and I wanted to get back to inspect our wagon, for it was a surprise for you, but I didn't expect you to come here so soon.'

'I couldn't keep away,' I told him.

'My precious wife,' he said, holding me close once more.

'Can we walk in the meadow?' I asked him, having a sudden desire to see the poppies.

'Very well,' he agreed. 'I can see that you are in a wilful mood.'

Kane put his arm around my shoulder as we walked once more through the woods and then into the meadow. I stopped and looked around me at the poppies whose petals were decorated with tiny raindrops. It was, indeed, wet underfoot and the hem of my dress was getting wet, but I ignored it for I was with Kane in our field.

'Dance with me!' I said suddenly.

'But there are no butterflies,' he observed.

'There will be' I assured him.

Taking me in his arms with his strong hand gently at my waist, we danced round and round and lo and behold, as we danced and I prayed for a butterfly, one appeared as if from nowhere to light our way. The Red Admiral flew around us for several seconds and then vanished.

'You are a sorceress,' Kane said as we both stopped dancing.

'Kane, I cannot go back to Northcliffe,' I told him, 'I am no longer happy there.'

'But you must, dear heart, for both our sakes.'

'No, I cannot. It is my aunt. She makes me feel uncomfortable and said there is something my dear uncle must tell me.'

'Please try to put up with it for a little longer, for me,' Kane pleaded.

'I cannot,' I protested, the tears starting to fall.

As we walked back to the clearing, my tears turned to sobs, for I was happy here and this was where I wished to be.

'Whatever is the matter?' Tessa asked coming over to me and placing an arm around me, pulling me close to her, but I could not speak.

'She doesn't wish to go back to the cottage,' Kane explained.

'Why not, Kate, tell me,' Tessa urged kindly.

'Because,' I sobbed, 'my aunt dislikes me and I feel uncomfortable in her presence. I can endure it no longer.'

'Also,' Kane added, 'her aunt says there is something her uncle must tell her.'

'Indeed, there is,' Tessa agreed. 'I've had enough of secrets and lies. Just one moment while I step into the wagon.'

She appeared again in no time, with her beautiful shawl around her shoulders and something wrapped in her hands. 'Come' she said. 'Come, Katherine, and you, Kane. We are to go to Northcliffe and sort this out once and for all.'

10

As I walked across the cliff with Kane and Tessa, his mother's words kept popping into my head 'secrets and lies'. What secrets and lies? What would Tessa know about them? I was curious as to what was in the package that she carried under her arm.

Kane stopped for a moment, but Tessa had determination in her steps, causing him to call after her.

'Mother. Please stop!' he urged. 'Are you sure you are doing the right thing? It doesn't matter to me, but what of Kate?'

I was even more perplexed.

'It has to be done, Kane, for both your sakes. I have stayed silent for long enough,' Tessa told him and then she walked on once more, Kane striding after her, his arm around my waist.

'What is going on?' I asked, more bemused than ever at the whole situation. Then, my aunt's words sprang to mind, 'what would she think if you tell her the truth'. What truth, and how was Tessa involved in this truth?

'It is the white cottage ahead, isn't it?' Tessa called out to me.

'It is,' I answered, very much afraid as to what may happen if Aunt Phoebe saw the three of us walk up her path.

It was Tessa who unlatched the gate. The sun was now high in the sky and I was very hot. My cheeks flushed as we walked up the path. Tessa raised her hand towards the brass knocker, Kane reaching for her hand, trying to delay her.

'Are you sure, Mother?' he pleaded.

'I am, I assure you.'

As Kane released her arm, Tessa lifted the knocker, banging it three times on the door. It seemed no sooner had she knocked, when Aggie appeared, looking aghast when she saw the three of us standing on the doorstep.

'Is your Mistress home?' Tessa asked quite calmly.

'She is,' Aggie replied, her voice quivering, 'but she has a visitor.'

'Please tell her that Tessa O'Brien wishes to speak with her,' Tessa said gently.

It was too late for Aggie to relay the message, for Aunt Phoebe had stepped into the hallway.

'What is the commotion, Aggie?' she demanded, then peered around the door and saw the three of us standing there. 'Katherine, come in.'

'I wish to speak with you,' Tessa said in a firm tone.

'Well, I do not wish to speak with you,' my aunt retorted.

'Leave her,' Kane said stepping between us.

'How dare you come to my doorstep and tell me what to do!' Aunt Phoebe said indignantly, stepping back from the doorway.

'Are you going to ask us in, or shall we air our dirty linen on your doorstep?' Tessa asked calmly.

'I have a visitor,' my aunt replied quietly.

'No matter,' Tessa persisted. 'This won't take long.'

'Call my husband,' my aunt instructed Aggie and as she scuttled off to do as she was bid.

Aunt Phoebe stood in the doorway, arms folded across the purple gown she had worn to church that morning. I had just watched the whole scene with fear in my heart.

'Let us go,' I urged Kane just as my uncle appeared behind Aunt Phoebe, with Constance Trevartha beside him.

'Whatever is amiss?' my dear uncle asked.

'I wish to talk with you and your wife,' Tessa told him, 'but not on your doorstep.'

Constance's face paled. 'I will leave,' she told my Aunt.

'No,' Tessa said, raising her voice. 'I wish you to hear what I have to say also.'

My Aunt put her hands to her face in despair.

'Ask them in, Phoebe,' my uncle coaxed.

My Aunt disappeared into the drawing room, Constance Trevartha following behind her.

'Please come in, the three of you,' Uncle Zac invited.

Carrying the mysterious parcel, Tessa stepped over the threshold of Northcliffe, followed by Kane and myself. As we stepped into the drawing room, Uncle Zac urged Tessa to sit down. Kane and I sat alongside her on the settle, with my aunt and Constance on the opposite one.

'Now you have lured your way into our home,' Aunt Phoebe began, 'maybe you will be so kind as to explain why you are here and then you may go.'

At these words, Tessa unwrapped the parcel she was carrying and placed the contents on the table. I gasped with amazement.

'It is my keepsake box, but I thought . . .'

'No, Katherine, it is my keepsake box,' Tessa interrupted. 'Please go and fetch yours and we will wait for you.'

I did as I was asked and on reaching my room, I could see that my beautiful box was, indeed, on the dressing table where I had left it. Hurrying back down the stairs and into the drawing room once more, I placed my keepsake box beside Tessa's.

'They are identical,' I said quietly as Uncle Zac leaned forward in the armchair to look more closely, noting the boxes were just the same, from the exquisite roses on the lid to the tiny pink hearts intertwined with the gilding.

'Katherine has gypsy blood in her veins, doesn't she?' Tessa asked.

For a moment, there was a deathly silence before my aunt spoke.

'How on earth can you come to this conclusion, from the ownership of a keepsake box?' she demanded, her eyes never leaving the contents of the table.

'I will show you,' Tessa replied, reaching across for her exquisite box. Lifting the lid, she removed the contents then felt along the back of the base, and I heard a click. As if by magic, Tessa lifted out the interior of the box and reaching inside, she drew out a small crocheted baby jacket decorated with pink ribbon.

'Now, if I am correct, the same thing will happen to Kate's box,' she explained.

I was mesmerised as she put the contents of my box on the table before her, then reaching for the secret lever, she then lifted out the contents with a flourish, and sure enough, she held a small crocheted baby's jacket in her hand. It was identical to the first one and edged with pink ribbon, the same ribbon which was lying on the top of my keepsake box.

'Who was my mother?' I asked Tessa.

'She was my sister, Katarina,' Tessa revealed.

The room was silent. Uncle Zac got up and walked over to the window.

'Tell her!' my aunt almost screamed, breaking the silence, as all that had been told me whirled around in my brain.

I was of gypsy blood, I thought, amazed at this revelation, but understanding why I was so drawn to the gypsy way of life.

'Tell her,' my aunt repeated, more calmly this time.

Uncle Zac approached me.

'This isn't easy to say . . . but . . . I am your father, Katherine,' he said quietly as a small tear ran down his cheek.

'My father!' I exclaimed. 'But how could this be?' I reached out for his hand and held on to it tightly.

'When I was betrothed to your aunt, the gypsies camped where they are now, and every day I would walk to the clearing to catch a glimpse of Katarina,' he began. 'We fell deeply in love with each other and one day we married in the clearing and jumping the broom, exactly as you and Kane did.

'My family were furious and forced me to let Katarina go. I married your aunt, but a few months later, Katarina appeared on our doorstep, heavy with child. She begged your aunt to let her have her baby in the cottage and you were born in this house, Katherine. But your mother died having lost a lot of blood.

'Your Aunt Phoebe agreed to bring you up here, making me promise that I would never tell you the circumstances of your birth. But now it has come out in the open, through no fault of my own.'

'This is why you let Kane and I marry?' I asked, the truth dawning on me.

'You are right, Katherine. When I knew that you, too, had jumped the broom, I only wanted you to be happy and share your life with the person you loved. I am not ashamed to say that I loved your mother, but I have a loyalty to my wife.'

'Loyalty,' my aunt scoffed.

'There isn't a day I haven't thought of Katarina,' my father admitted. 'Please say you understand,' he pleaded.

I got up and put my arms around him.

'Of course I do,' I whispered. I turned to Aunt Phoebe. 'And I thank you for bringing me up as you did, Aunt.'

'This does not mean that I give you my blessing,' Aunt Phoebe said.

'Maybe you will when I tell you something else,' Tessa said.

'There is nothing you can possibly tell me that would make me change my mind,' my Aunt replied resolutely.

'What if I were to tell you that Kane is a son of Treverrick?' Tessa revealed, looking at Constance Trevartha as she spoke.

'A son of Treverrick!' my aunt exclaimed, looking at Constance. 'Neither I nor Jed are this young man's parents and he knows it,' Tessa said.

'Then who does he belong to?' Aunt Phoebe asked incredulously.

There was a moment's pause until Constance spoke.

'Patience,' she whispered. 'He belongs to Patience.'

'What?' my aunt asked in utter shock.

'It is true,' Constance began. 'My

sister gave birth to a little boy, out of wedlock, and we asked Jed and Tessa if they would raise him as their own, in order to avoid scandal. Patience was sent to France for quite some time and only recently returned.'

'You knew of this, Kane?' I asked, looking to him for an answer.

'Tessa told me when I was younger, but I was happy living the gypsy way of life. I would never want to change that,' he admitted.

'So what say you now?' Tessa asked of my aunt, who sat with an ashen face.

'I . . . Perhaps I could support this marriage under the circumstances,' she meekly replied.

'So you would judge a man on the circumstance of his birth and not the person himself?' Tessa queried.

'It would appear so,' my aunt replied, 'I could not bear Katherine to do what her father did twenty years ago and ruin her life.'

'I will look after Kate and cherish her for the rest of our lives, but I will not give up my way of life,' Kane said emphatically.

'I do understand your dilemma now, Aunt,' I told her.

'I take it you two young people are to marry?' Constance asked.

'We have jumped the broom already,' Kane revealed, 'but we are now in the process of marrying in church, if it is to be allowed.'

'I guessed as much when the banns were called this morning. I must admit to being happy for my nephew, for he couldn't be marrying a lovelier young woman,' she kindly said.

'Thank you, Mrs Trevartha,' I responded with a grateful heart.

'What problem have you marrying in the church?' my aunt's friend asked.

'I am not of your religion, which could be a stumbling block,' Kane told her.

'I think I can help you there,' Constance said. 'Before we handed Kane over to Tessa and Jed, he was baptised in the church one morning. It must be on their records.'

I looked at Kane with sparkling eyes, for at last luck was with us.

'That is good fortune,' Kane said, looking at me. 'It would seem at last, we can be together.'

'And will you give these two young people who are so in love, your blessing now?' my father asked Aunt Phoebe.

She looked down at her lap for a moment. 'I have no reason not to.'

I breathed a big sigh of relief.

Aggie brought us a tray of tea and cake as requested by my aunt. While I sipped my tea, I mulled over the recent revelations. It must have been hard for my aunt to carry such a secret for twenty years and I could now understand why she was so against my union with Kane. I could hardly believe that Kane was Patience's son, but I was so glad Tessa had insisted on coming to Northcliffe today, for I had found a father and was now free to marry Kane. I lifted up the baby coat.

'Who gave you and your sister the

keepsake boxes?' I asked.

'Our mother, not long before she died,' Tessa told me. 'I knew as soon as I saw the one belonging to you, that it was my sister's.'

'You are my aunt,' I declared.

'Yes, I am,' she told me.

'Was my mother beautiful?' I asked.

'She was very beautiful, you are a lot like her, Katherine,' Tessa replied. 'I am so pleased that you and Kane have fallen in love with each other. You were meant to be together.'

'That is true,' Kane said, smiling at me.

I agreed, at my aunt's request, to stay at Northcliffe until my marriage to Kane. Each day I walked to the clearing, sometimes with Aggie, and she helped me to prepare the *vardo* for Kane and I to live in.

Tessa taught me to crochet and before long, I was crocheting my own sheets, which Aunt Phoebe had kindly given to us. She had, at last, come around to the idea of Kane and I marrying. She was disappointed when I insisted I wear my cream skirt and orange blouse on my wedding day, but I wanted to look as I had on the day Kane and I had jumped the broom. I knew that the ceremony in the clearing was the one I would acknowledge all my life, but I would marry in church for Aunt Phoebe's sake.

'I wish to carry a bouquet of poppies,' I told Kane the day before we were due to marry at the church.

It was a glorious, sunny day and we had been sorting out our possessions and putting them away in the *vardo*. The beautiful keepsake box was pride of place as I laid it on the chest. I ran my hand over the beautiful pink roses, feeling very close to my mother.

My father had told me that Katarina had given it to Aunt Phoebe before she died and made her promise it would be handed over to me when I was of an age to appreciate it.

When we had finished in the wagon, we shared a cup of tea with Tessa then walked through the wood together, hand in hand. It was so peaceful that I could hear the stream trickling across the stones. A blackbird sang and we stopped to listen, both enraptured by the sound.

Then, we stepped into the poppy meadow once more. There weren't quite as many blooms as there had been on the first day we had walked this way, but enough for me to fashion a bouquet to carry as I walked down the aisle the next day. I caught Kane looking back at Treverrick, the walls of which looked softer and more inviting somehow.

'A penny for your thoughts,' I told him.

'I was just thinking that I can hardly believe I was born at the big house and am indeed a Treverrick.'

'Are you wishing that you lived there?' I asked him.

'Definitely not,' he told me. 'I like the free and easy life I have, travelling the country, working in the orchards and waking each morning to the sound of the birds in the trees. What about you?' he asked, taking me in his arms and with one hand, freeing the pins from my hair, which then tumbled down my back in a cascade of black waves.

'All I wish for, is to be with you and wake each morning in your arms,' I told him, reaching up a hand and stroking his cheek.

'That is all I need to hear,' he replied.

We danced together amongst the poppies in the meadow, holding each other close, our hearts beating as one. Magically, three Red Admiral butterflies started to flutter around us and we danced.

THE END

We do hope that you have enjoyed reading this large print book.

Did you know that all of our titles are available for purchase?

We publish a wide range of high quality large print books including:
Romances, Mysteries, Classics
General Fiction
Non Fiction and Westerns

Special interest titles available in large print are:
The Little Oxford Dictionary
Music Book, Song Book
Hymn Book, Service Book

Also available from us courtesy of Oxford University Press:
Young Readers' Dictionary
(large print edition)
Young Readers' Thesaurus
(large print edition)

For further information or a free brochure, please contact us at:
Ulverscroft Large Print Books Ltd.,
The Green, Bradgate Road, Anstey,
Leicester, LE7 7FU, England.
Tel: (00 44) **0116 236 4325**
Fax: (00 44) **0116 234 0205**

Other titles in the
Linford Romance Library:

RACHEL'S COMING HOME

Gillian Villiers

When her parents run into difficulties running their boarding kennels, Rachel Collington decides to resign from her job and return home to help out. The first customer she encounters is arrogant Philip Milligan, who is nowhere near as friendly as his two collies. Gradually though, he begins to thaw — but just as Rachel is wondering if she has misjudged him, it seems that someone is intent on sabotaging the Kennels' reputation.

HEALING LOVE

Cara Cooper

Dr James Frayne's personal life is in meltdown and it is beginning to affect his work. Becky, his Practice Manager, is deeply concerned and wants to help. But Dr James cannot afford to let her in on his secret — if she discovers what's troubling him, it could lose him his job. When his cold efficiency and her powers of deduction collide, sparks fly and emotions are stirred — changing both their lives forever . . .

ANGEL HARVEST

Glenis Wilson

Jennifer Dunbar's dream of becoming a successful lady jockey seems to be over when she has to quit to look after Ellie, her three-year-old niece. Ellie's mother, Rosamund, was killed during a thunderstorm. Mystery surrounds her death — and the identity of Ellie's father. Jennifer is determined to find him. But her search impacts upon other people, threatening to destroy not only their lives, but also her own. Then Jennifer discovers — too late — some secrets should remain secret . . .

FORTUNES OF WAR

Jasmina Svenne

Since being orphaned, Lucy Prior
has led a quiet life with her brother
and his family on their farm in
upstate New York. Now though, that
peaceful existence is threatened by
the approach of the American War of
Independence. Even so, when she
stumbles upon a handsome stranger
hiding in the byre, Lucy cannot
resist shielding him from his pursu-
ers. But her actions will have
far-reaching consequences — not
only for herself, but also for the
whole of her family.

AT THE END OF THE RAINBOW

Wendy Kremer

Alex is escaping from an unhappy love affair. She finds employment helping Julian to finish writing his latest book. Julian is partially paralysed, and confined to a wheelchair — the result of a car accident in which his wife was killed. He could improve — perhaps even restore — his mobility by accepting new medical treatment. But he goes on punishing himself. Can Alex and Julian forget the past, and find a future together?

BLIGHTED INHERITANCE

Anne Hewland

Following her father's murder, Leonora Mayfield disguises herself as a maid-servant in order to seek proof of a large amount of money owed by her father's employer, Sir Francis Carrock. She is determined to dislike and distrust her father's successor, Adam Rigton, but her search proves more difficult than expected and she is reluctantly becoming attracted to Adam. Is there more than a debt at stake and has she unknowingly placed herself and younger brother, Robert, in grave danger?